"You better have a plan beyond this moment," Nikki whispered fervently to Evan, "because in about five minutes, my entire family is going to believe we're sleeping together."

He nodded. "We have a few options," he murmured back.

"What are they?"

"I can say I was kidding. But that would make me look weird, and I have an image to uphold."

"Option two?"

"You could wait a few days, then tell your family you realized you're just not that into me."

"And make them worry even more, because now they think I'm rash and erratic? Next option."

"We let it ride. And we bear in mind that we told only a partial lie."

"How do you figure?"

With her still glued to his side for Gia's sake, Evan glanced down at her. "It pains me that you have to ask."

"What?"

He shook his head. "That forgettable, was it? I'm referring to the fact that we did sleep together. Once." Lowering his head, he added even more softly, "And speaking for myself, I thought we were damn successful at putting the *whoop* in *whoopee*."

Dear Reader,

As I write this, I'm celebrating the thirtieth anniversary of my first sale to Harlequin. Writing romance novels has yielded many gifts, not the least of which has been the chance to make lifelong friends who share the love of storytelling—and coffee. I married my best friend during that time, too. There's a theme here: friendship sets the roots of happiness deep into the earth.

In *Forever, Plus One*, Nikki and Evan have already tried romance and decided to remain strictly platonic. They'll be each other's BFF and plus-one when the occasion warrants, but that's as far as they plan to take it.

Since when does the heart obey the head?

There's a wonderful Yiddish word—*beshert*. It means "destiny" and is typically used to refer to the person who becomes our soul mate. The soul, though, is a funny thing. We enter the world with it, and we leave with it, but connecting to our soul and our soul's desire can be tricky while we're here. We can meet our destiny yet not recognize it immediately, or realize that even "meant to be" can take a lot of work!

I hope you're blessed with friends, family, work and the mate who feeds your soul. And I thank you from the bottom of my heart for allowing me to be part of your bookshelf for thirty years!

Blessings,

Wendy

Forever, Plus One

WENDY WARREN

HARLEQUIN
SPECIAL
EDITION

HARLEQUIN®
SPECIAL EDITION™

Recycling programs for this product may not exist in your area.

ISBN-13: 978-1-335-72414-4

Forever, Plus One

Copyright © 2022 by Wendy Warren

For questions and comments about the quality of this book, please contact us at CustomerService@Harlequin.com.

Harlequin Enterprises ULC
22 Adelaide St. West, 41st Floor
Toronto, Ontario M5H 4E3, Canada
www.Harlequin.com

Printed in U.S.A.

Wendy Warren loves to write about ordinary people who find extraordinary love. Laughter, family and close-knit communities figure prominently, too. Her books have won two Romance Writers of America RITA® Awards and have been nominated for numerous others. She lives in the Pacific Northwest with human and nonhuman critters who don't read nearly as much as she'd like, but they sure do make her laugh and feel loved.

Books by Wendy Warren

Harlequin Special Edition

Holliday, Oregon

Moonlight, Menorahs and Mistletoe

The Men of Thunder Ridge

Do You Take This Baby?
Kiss Me, Sheriff!
His Surprise Son

Home Sweet Honeyford

Caleb's Bride
Something Unexpected
The Cowboy's Convenient Bride
Once More, At Midnight

Logan's Legacy Revisited

The Baby Bargain

Visit the Author Profile page
at Harlequin.com for more titles.

After my father—a marine, history buff
and tough businessman—passed away,
I discovered he kept a file of my romance novels,
book reviews and interviews. I had no idea.

My mother read everything I wrote
(many more times than I did!) and often
came up with fabulous book ideas.

They left this earth far too soon,
but they've never left me.

Thanks, Mom and Dad.

Chapter One

Makeup perfectly intact (no runny mascara): *Check.*

Expression Zen and contented, suggesting radical acceptance of current circumstances: *Check.*

Hair washed and styled as if she gave a crap and body looking toned as hell despite large bag of Chicago corn and pint of pistachio gelato consumed during previous night's pity party: *Check, check.*

Okay, ready as I'll ever be.

Nikki took a deep breath, blew it out and flipped her car visor up, closing the mirror. With a broad smile enhanced by the copious use of Crest White-strips during the past ten months, she exited her vehicle and stepped into the soft sunshine of an

April afternoon in the elegant Eastmoreland district of Portland, Oregon. Her parents had already been to Saturday Torah study and morning services and were expecting their kids and kids' partners, including her and Drew, for their once-a-month Shabbat *mishpachah* (translation: Extreme Family) luncheon. Nikki had texted yesterday to let her mom know that Drew Northrup, to whom she had become engaged ten months ago, would not be joining them today, not that it would alter her mother's meal plans one iota. Drew, personal trainer and certified food coach, ate only organic, grass-fed organ meats these days. Nikki's parents were kosher vegetarians.

Walking up Rivka and Sang Choi's flower-lined walkway, Nikki nodded to her mother's village of ceramic lawn elves. Not gnomes—Rivka was *very* clear about that. Necklaces made from apple seeds, left by "fairies" for the local kids, decorated two dwarf Japanese maples. Flanking the front-porch steps were matching boxwoods shaped like elephants with their trunks raised. Rivka's landscaping was fine if you lived in Walt Disney World, but in Eastmoreland, the Choi family was considered more than a little offbeat.

Many homes in the neighborhood crept into the million-dollar range and above, but Rivka and Sang had moved to Eastmoreland for the respected neighborhood schools and purchased the one home they'd

been able to afford at the time—a nineteen fifties
daylight ranch with enough bedrooms for their three
kids and an ample yard they'd filled with all man-
ner of childhood fun.

The Choi chicks had long ago flown the coop,
yet the house remained as distinct and cheerful as
ever. Unfortunately, today Nikki felt more sick-
to-her-stomach than cheery. Could be due to last
night's binge; could be the fear that she was going
to burst into tears at any moment, thereby send-
ing her mother into paroxysms of worry over her
eldest child.

Passing the In This House, We Believe... sign
nestled in a brick planter filled with her mother's
impatiens, Nikki climbed the porch steps—only
two, but today it felt like twenty. After touching
the multicolored glass mezuzah affixed to her parents' doorpost, she brought her fingers to her lips.

Help me not to cry, God. That's all I ask today.
Reaching toward the doorbell, she added under her
breath, "And please don't let anyone else cry, and
also let me keep my dignity and be a good, kind and
not bitter person, and please help my reproductive
system to function ten years younger than it actually
is so this isn't the end of all my hopes and dreams.
Thank you very much. Amen." She gave the doorbell a hard jab and waited.

"Lev, get the door!" she heard her mother call to
her brother inside the house, and several seconds

later, Lev Hanwool Choi opened the door, his familiar grin a balm to her aching spirit.

"Annyeonghaseyo," he greeted in Korean, following with the Hebrew salutation for Saturday, "Shabbat shalom."

Unlike her, Lev was a homegrown Choi, born three years after she had been adopted by their Jewish Franco American mother and South Korean American dad. Also unlike her, he had fairly pale skin, though he did share her dark hair and height disadvantage. Lev had topped out at five feet five inches, taking after their mother's side of the family. Nikki had studied dance all through school, and when her posture was excellent, she managed to eke out a scant half inch over five feet.

"Have I ever told you how pretentious you sound when you open a door with multiple international greetings?" Stepping across the threshold, she hugged her sibling.

"I have an affinity for world languages."

"And a membership to Rosetta Stone. Which I think you're abusing."

He *tsked* at her. "You're just jealous."

That was probably true. Even after listening to their father's native tongue most of her life, she barely spoke any Korean. Ditto Hebrew even with years of Hebrew school under her belt, and double ditto Spanish despite three long, miserable years of it in high school. Languages were not her thing.

She glanced around. "Where are my unpretentious sister-in-law and innocent niece?"

"In the guest room. June's breastfeeding Lani."

The image of her sweet sister-in-law sharing that special bonding time with their four-month-old created a painful pull on Nikki's heart, made worse when Lev stuck his head out the door and asked, "Where's your other half?"

It was shocking how quickly the tears could come. They stung Nikki's eyes like smog. She turned before Lev could see them. "Is everyone here?" She wanted to tell the family her news one time and one time only.

No sooner had she spoken than the sound of galloping feet made her look to her left, where the most charming six-year-old on the planet (as far as she was concerned) raced toward her.

"Aunt Nikki!" he exclaimed, cannonballing into her arms, which seemed always to open automatically when Noah was around.

"Noah! I didn't realize you were going to be here," she said, hugging tightly as she swept him off the floor and jiggled him around, which he adored. As always, he felt so good in her arms, and she hung on a little extra today.

"Me and my dad got invited."

"My dad and I," corrected the dad in question, who, unfortunately for Noah, happened to teach

English Language Arts to middle schoolers and was currently sporting a black T-shirt that read:

Let's eat, kids!

Let's eat kids!

See how important punctuation is?

"We were invited two weeks ago," Evan Northrup said as he approached Nikki, before kissing her cheek.

"Oh yeah, that's right." She nodded weakly, having completely forgotten. Holy crud fudgeknuckles. Evan and Drew Northrup, the man to whom she'd been engaged for ten months, were brothers. As different as a meandering country road and a five-lane highway, they were nonetheless blood relations and may have spoken in the past couple of days. Did Evan already know what she'd come here to say this afternoon? Might he—heaven forbid—be aware of the humiliating details?

Searching Evan's features over the top of his son's chestnut-colored head, she tried to discern whether he'd already heard that she had been dumped, but Evan wasn't tipping his hand.

With his customary happy expression and a face that looked like the living definition of wholesome, he smiled at her as he tousled his son's soft hair. "Aunt Rivka told me she needs a frosting tester for the cake she baked," he told the boy. "It's chocolate with candy inside. Yuck, right? I told her I don't know anyone here who will want to taste *that*, but we could go outside and look around for someone."

"Dad!" Twisting in Nikki's arms, Noah put his hands on either side of his father's face. "*I* will want to taste that cake. 'Specially, I want to taste the *candy*." When he wriggled to get down, Evan took him from Nikki and set his feet on the floor. "I gotta tell Aunt Rivka myself," Noah exclaimed. With the same velocity he used to enter the foyer, the little boy ran to the kitchen.

"Chocolate with candy inside," Lev complained. "She used to make carrot cake with cream cheese frosting. *My* favorite."

"Are you really resenting a six-year-old right now?" Nikki asked.

"No, but I am going to see if I can bribe him to tell Mom he wants carrot cake next time." Lev sauntered off after Noah.

"Hard to believe he's a licensed therapist," she said fondly to Evan, watching her brother leave.

"I like your brother." Evan turned his megawatt grin on her. "So what have you been doing with your week, Nicolette?" he asked as they wandered toward the living room.

"Oh…you know." Evan was incapable of guile, which meant it was quite likely he really didn't know what had happened. "Have you seen Drew this week?"

"No, I was out of town, remember? Took my eighth graders to Ashland to see some theater."

"Right, I forgot."

"Ach." He winced. "Doomed to be forgettable." Though he wagged his head with exaggerated resignation, the sparkle never left his clear-sky eyes.

"You are not forgettable. You are anything but forgettable." It was true. She loved Evan. Everyone did. It was also true that Evan Northrup was less forcefully charismatic than his baby brother, who possessed the larger-than-life dynamism that bred success stories. Currently Drew was busy parlaying his charisma and love of the spotlight into a six-figure fitness career. And that was only the beginning of what he intended to do. Drew was a lightning strike. Evan was more…spring sunshine.

Nikki had met Evan Northrup two years ago at an educator's workshop on equity. Assigned to the same small discussion group, they'd discovered they worked in the same district. She'd been struck quickly by his integrity, intelligence and willingness to discuss all points of view. A good guy—that's what she'd thought of Evan Northrup at the time. He hadn't had a blog or YouTube channel (still didn't); he'd just wanted to become a better teacher.

He'd seemed to like her, too, right off the bat, asking her to join him at lunch, trading numbers at the end of the workshop and, later, introducing her to his brother Drew.

Nikki had fallen hard and fast for the younger Northrup brother. The first time they'd met, in fact—at the community July Fourth celebration where Evan had directed a middle-school recitation of the Declaration of Independence and Drew had set up a booth to promote his personal training business, LeanUp With NorthrUp. Nikki had joined them for lunch at Evan's invitation, and as Evan himself later noted while toasting them at their engagement party, "It was hard to tell whether there were more fireworks in the sky or between you two crazy kids."

Drew worked all year round, building his business, whereas she and Evan were already settled into their careers—she as a high school guidance counselor, and he as a teacher. They both had summer, winter and spring breaks off, so Drew had been A-OK with his brother and his best girl hanging out together when he wasn't available. She and Evan lived a short drive from each other in Holliday, Oregon, which was about an hour south of where Drew was based in Portland. Evan had become the male friend-without-benefits all her single girlfriends wished they had—available on weekends for fun (his adorable son being a bonus) when Drew was working, and ready for grown-up talk on weeknights after Noah's bedtime. He laughed easily, listened patiently, and as far as she could tell his only flaw was being way too picky when it came to dating.

"I'd ask how your date with Alyssa went, but I already heard," Nikki mentioned now, eliciting a rueful smile. "You shouldn't be smiling," she admonished. "I set you up with my hairstylist, and you ended the date at eight thirty! Now I'm going to have to find a new hair salon, and I love my hair salon." Tilting her head, she narrowed her eyes at him. "So what was wrong this time, dude? Alyssa used double negatives? Didn't know who wrote *The Scarlet Letter*?"

Pressing his lips together, Evan snapped his fingers. "Damn it, I knew I forgot to ask her something."

"I'm going to stop setting you up."

"Promise?"

Nikki wagged her head. "You're looking for perfection. It doesn't exist."

"I'm not looking for anything. I keep telling you that. Although I recall you mentioning once that Drew is perfect."

Had she? The pinched feeling in her chest returned. She probably had said something idiotic like that. Lord knew she'd tried hard enough and long enough to believe they were perfect together.

Ten months ago, after Drew proposed to her on the ski lift at Mount Hood, Nikki had made her fastest run ever to the bottom of the mountain, champing at the bit to call Evan and tell him to get ready to play best man. She'd handed Drew the phone so Evan could congratulate his brother and then grabbed it back to ask Evan if he would still hang out with her when she was "a boring married woman."

"Of course. As far as I'm concerned, I'm not losing a friend—I'm gaining a great babysitter." His voice had held the humor she loved so much. "And now you'll be Noah's aunt forever." That had made her feel immensely relieved and sincerely delighted. She couldn't wait to add her and Drew's kids to the mix and, yes, had pictured a "perfect" life absolutely drenched in love.

On top of the awfulness of splitting from the man with whom she'd planned to spend her life, there was now the awfulness of wondering whether everything between her and Evan would change. Would he have to take sides? People almost always did when they were close to both partners in a breakup.

Damn the waterworks; she felt herself tearing up again.

"Hey, Choi," Evan said. When she looked at him, he was studying her intently. "You okay?"

Good lord, she had to get this over with! Tell everyone what was happening and move on with her life, come what may. "I'm fine. Hay fever's acting up. Do you know where my dad is?"

"In the kitchen making Sex-On-The-Beach Slushies in his new blender while your mother reprimands him for saying 'the sex word,' as she calls it, in front of my six-year-old. Every time she says, 'Sang! Stop saying the sex word in front of the c-h-i-l-d,' your father and brother laugh like hyenas."

Closing her eyes, Nikki shook her head. "I'm so sorry."

"Are you kidding? I live for this. Beats the heck out of Northrup House." Which was how he referred to the Lake Oswego mini-manse where his father and stepmother resided. "They think they're living on the edge when they give the housekeeper the night off."

"They're not that bad." She grabbed his arm. "Let's go to the kitchen."

"Sure." He seemed only slightly bemused as she abandoned the walk to the living room and turned them in the opposite direction. "So, summer break is only a month away," he commented. "I'm thinking of taking Noah on a tour of Oregon, all the kid-friendly hot spots. Brilliant idea, or too much too soon?"

Nikki summoned a smile, but she felt shaky as jelly inside. "No, that would be fun. He's a good little traveler."

"That he is. I'll start with his favorites—Oaks Park and water slide runs—then ease him into the High Desert Museum and the Painted Hills."

Evan was such a good, good father. Taught eighth grade—never an easy task—yet always had plenty of energy for his son. Weekends and school breaks were devoted to his child. He'd been single parenting almost since Noah was born.

Gently, Evan bumped her shoulder. "Thanks for saying yes every time Noah asked you to come with us to Oaks Park last summer."

"Are you kidding?" she said, summoning a brightness she didn't feel. "Thirty-two times on the Tilt-A-Whirl in eight weeks? I wouldn't have missed it. I hardly threw up at all the last five rides."

Evan laughed, managing to make the sound rueful and grateful at the same time. "You were a great sport." Lowering his head and raising his gaze to meet hers, a move that made him look irresistibly boyish, he said, "Listen, I'd ask if you want to see the Painted Hills with us this summer, but I figure you've got a honeymoon and some newlywedded bliss to take care of, so—"

He stopped abruptly. Probably due to the alarming squeak that emerged through her closed lips.

"Nikki." His happy eyes grew uncharacteristically serious as he held her upper arms, halting their progress toward the kitchen. "Hey." His voice was gentle as a feather. "What's wrong?"

Pressing her fingers to her lips, she shook her head. He'd been her friend before becoming her brother-in-law-to-be, and she hoped with all her heart that he would remain her good friend after what she was about to say. Worry that he might feel the need to choose sides or simply drift out of her life—taking the incredible Noah along with him—engulfed her.

"Nik—"

"Is that my girl?" Sang Choi strode into the dining room, carrying the glass jar of his prized KitchenAid K400 blender. "Look at this! S-E-X-On-The-Beach Slushies. I didn't even have to pour it through a sieve. That's how good this blender is."

"Can you make me a virgin SOTB?" Lev's wife, June, asked as she entered from the hallway, tiny baby Lani in her arms. "Hi, Nik. Want to hold your niece? She's all fed and changed."

Hold a perfect infant whose every gurgle and coo made Nikki yearn so strongly for a baby of her own that she'd been trying to convince Drew they should toss her birth control ASAP? Bad idea at the moment.

"You know—" she began to decline only to be interrupted by her mother, Rivka, who marched in from the kitchen like the five-foot-four-inch whirl-wind she was.

"Sang!" Rivka said in her most reprimanding tone. "Stop saying sex on the b-e-a-c-h when there are c-h-i-l-d-r-e-n in the house. It isn't appropriate."

June and Evan hid their smiles.

Sang shrugged. "OK, Mama, whatever you say."

Nikki loved her family. They were a little loopy,

but loving and loyal and wonderful, too. Her mother and father were *thrilled* to be grandparents. The thought of having a baby—babies—of her own and raising them here in the midst of the joyful chaos… Lately, that thought had made every day brighter, every annoyance insignificant. Now she was nearly thirty-seven, fiancé-less and afraid menopause would arrive before the stork.

"Nikki. Sweetheart." Rushing toward her, Rivka peered closely at her elder daughter. "Honey, what's wrong? Are you crying?"

"No. No, Mom. I'm fine," she lied, sucking in her emotions, determined to get through this day with dignity, if nothing else.

"Lev!" June hollered above her snoozing baby's head. "Come in here. Your sister is crying."

"I'm not." Once again, Nikki felt Evan's steadying hand, this time beneath her elbow. She turned her head. He had schooled his handsome hot-boy-next-door features into his teacher expression— calm and neutral, but ready to act.

Lev and Noah breezed into the living room from the kitchen, Noah smeared with chocolate and Lev popping Skittles in his mouth as he eyed his sister curiously. "What's up?"

Fudge. She'd had this planned. They would eat her mom's good food, everyone would be relaxed and she would make her announcement. *Folks, after careful consideration, Drew and I have amicably and* mutually *decided that we are not compatible enough to make a marriage last. With the wedding six weeks away, we realize the timing is terrible, yet we* concur *that it is far better to part now, without the added stress of legal entanglement. I am one hundred percent at peace with this* joint *decision.*

Her family would be shocked at first, of course, but they would recover. Everyone would recover.

"What's wrong, bubaleh?" Her father, who had converted to Judaism after meeting Rivka, yet knew more Yiddish than all her mother's relatives combined, stepped forward. At sixty-seven, Sang Choi's skin was still handsomely unlined, but he could project worry from thirty paces.

Change of plans. She would make her announcement before lunch, telling them about her canceled wedding (oh, Lord, the tropical honeymoon, too) while they were in the living room sipping Sex-On-The-Beach Slushies. Which, if you thought about it was a poetically Instagrammable moment.

"Mom," she began, "Dad. Everyone…" *Let's go into the living room.* That's what she was about to say. Calmly. Dispassionately. But then, before Nikki could stop herself, she blurted, "Drew dumped me!" and burst into tears.

Sobs, actually.

"What!"

"When was this?"

"Oh, sweetie, no!"

"That *ass*."

And then Evan said the F-word, but very softly.

Nikki covered her face with her hands while her shoulders heaved and awful sounds emerged from deep inside her—much louder than squeaks.

"Lev, hold the baby. Nikki, do you have a therapist?" June asked.

"Want some frosting, Aunt Nikki?" Noah urged. Oh, God bless him. She was probably frightening him. The thought made her sob harder.

"I'll get a box of tissues," her father said.

"I never trusted Drew! Imagine eating only organ meats, not even a vegetable. Whoever heard of such a thing? That *putz*." Those words were Rivka's, who quickly followed up with, "I'm sorry, Evan. No offense."

"None taken." His hand, firm and sure, retained its hold on Nikki's arm. "Why don't we all go into the living room and sit down." Ever the voice of reason, thank God.

They moved as a herd, as if by allowing little space around Nikki they could protect her from what had already befallen. Taking their places on her parents' sectional, Nikki felt Rivka burrow in on her left. Evan took a seat to her right, close enough for their knees to touch.

Nikki kept her head lowered, elbows on her thighs, hands still covering her face. This was not what she wanted, not *at all*. She had wanted to say little, make everyone believe she was fine, make *herself* believe she was fine and that breaking up six weeks—six stinkin' weeks!—before the wedding of her dreams was not a tragedy. No, it was a second chance to find the right person (never mind that her thirty-seventh birthday was around the corner and that the chances of finding a single man her age who was not intimacy phobic or suffering from erectile dysfunction were dwindling with every passing minute.)

Sang must have handed a box of tissues to Rivka, who tried to tuck a wad of them under Nikki's hands with the instruction, "Blow, sweetheart."

Raising her head, Nikki obliged, snuffling, "Thanks, Mom." As she wiped her eyes, she saw that a tall SOTB Slushy had been placed on the coffee table before her and that Noah had scrambled onto his daddy's lap.

"I'm sorry." She tried to smile at them all, but at Noah, especially. "I'm fine. Honestly, I am."

Noah nodded. "Daddy says it's brave to cry." He reached out to give her shoulder a pat. "You must be *really* brave, Aunt Nikki. Right, Dad?"

Evan's lake-colored eyes did not waver. "Yes. Aunt Nikki is the bravest person I know."

Whether or not he meant it, Nikki looked at Evan with the deepest gratitude. His eyes were understanding. Accepting.

What a good, good man.

I need to find him a woman he'll date more than once.

He and Noah were so wonderful, they shouldn't be alone. No one wonderful should be alone. No one mediocre should be alone, either. No one at all should be alone unless they wanted to be. And on that thought—

She burst into tears again.

Chapter Two

Leave it to Drew to screw up a romantic relationship. Correction: Leave it to every XY chromosome carrier in his family to screw up a romantic relationship. The XXs hadn't done so well, either.

Evan lifted his six-year-old son off his lap. Raising the boy as high as he could before setting his sneakered feet on the ground. "Okay, buddy boy, I think I spied a new tunnel slide out back. You know any kids who like tunnel slides?"

"Really? This kid likes tunnel slides!" Noah instantly forgot the adult conversation in favor of testing out the newest addition to the backyard playground structure Sang had been building since Lev and June showed everyone their ultrasound. A bit premature, perhaps, but Evan admired…maybe envied…their enthusiasm. His father and stepmother (who, FWIW, was younger than he was) considered a formal dinner followed by an explanation of how to build a savings account to be a fun night with the grandson.

Rivka and Sang invited Noah to romp on their ever-expanding play structure then thanked him for "breaking it in." Good folks, the Chois.

Knowing Nikki would never say anything unflattering about Noah's uncle in front of him, Evan started to rise so he could take his son outside.

Sang stood, extending a hand to Noah. "Come on, I'll show you the slide, plus a tire swing I just put up."

"Thanks, Mr. C!" Noah started to gallop toward Nikki's father, then stopped and remembered to ask, "Can I, Dad?"

"You sure?" Evan asked Sang, reluctant to take him from his daughter at this particular moment.

Sang waved away the concern. "You stay," he told the younger man. "It involves your brother, so you should hear the news sooner than later. Rivka will give me the instant replay." Taking Noah's hand, he allowed the little boy to lead him from the room. Noah was all chatter and easy joy despite the fog of concern that hung low over the room.

Rivka watched her daughter intently. With thick, wavy strawberry blond hair piled atop her head and

her refined features keen with anxious protective-
ness, she reminded him of a loving lioness.

Lev stood at the end of the sofa, arms crossed,
lips compressed as his wife, June, held their sleepy
baby, giving tiny Lani a series of bottom pats and
looking very much like she was trying to comfort
herself more than their blissfully unaware daughter.

The only member of the Choi family not present
was Gia, the youngest sibling. Evan had expected to
see her today, but under the circumstances, maybe
it was better that she was absent. Gia and Nikki
tended to see who could outcaretake the other, and
it seemed to Evan that clear, neutral heads needed
to prevail right now. Although, the idea that anyone
in this room was going to be neutral was…pretty
damn ridiculous.

Evan didn't know the details of Nikki's breakup.
Drew hadn't called, texted or otherwise given any
indication that something was wrong with his and
Nik's relationship. Drew and he were not confi-
dantes. Never had been. Evan had been five when
his father married Drew's mother, the first of his
four stepmothers (so far). Drew had been born a
year later, and at first Evan had welcomed the idea
of a brother, someone to whom he could feel close
and loyal to in a house where affection and loyalty
were in short supply.

It hadn't worked out that way. Evan's father and
stepmother had celebrated Drew's second birthday

by divorcing. Drew had lived with them part-time, and the family dynamics had led to some near-Biblical competitiveness between the brothers.

Still, they were blood relations. The desire to protect his younger bro, though it had grown faint over the years, persisted, and Evan was pretty certain Drew was about to get reamed. Probably deserved it, too, but Evan figured his presence might soften the blows.

He looked at Nikki, whose sobs had settled into something softer and more whimpering. She'd cried in front of him before. Nik led with her heart. She teared up over commercials, cried if she hurt her sister's feelings, sobbed when the pigeon they'd found wandering alone with a broken wing had gone to its reward despite their best efforts. Usually in the aftermath of an emotional storm, he tossed an arm around her shoulders or rubbed her back, then made her mac 'n' cheese like he did for Noah when he was upset.

Looked like it was going to take a hell of a lot more than noodles and a sharp cheddar to get her through this.

Starting with the arm around her shoulders, he turned slightly toward her, making his chest available as she leaned her head on him.

"Take some deep breaths," he murmured, modeling the same calming breathing technique he used with Noah—four count in, hold, four count out. He inhaled the scent of the coconut shampoo she loved, and very quickly they were breathing in unison.

Her body relaxed into him. A slight, sorrowful smile touched his lips.

When Nikki had first shown interest in Drew, he'd tried to warn her about his brother's less-sterling attributes—the competitiveness, the self-interest that lurked beneath the superficial charm. Problem was, her reaction when she'd first met Drew had been starry-eyed, a bit bashful, completely smitten. If he'd told her straight up Drew wasn't right for her, would she have believed him? Or, would he have looked like a jealous ass *and* possibly lost his best friend? He'd tried instead to keep an eye on his brother, to make sure Nikki was having a positive effect on him, rather than Drew having a negative effect on her.

Yes, Northrups sucked at romantic relationships—no point denying it; in that regard, he was a true Northrup, but he was a good dad and a good friend. He tried to be that good friend now.

"What happened?" he asked her softly. "How did it end?"

Nikki sniffled then blew her nose loudly. "We've been on different tracks for a while, and I guess I thought we'd get back on course. Eventually. In time for the wedding. But we didn't." She wagged her head sorrowfully. "Our tracks are too far apart."

"Are those Drew's words or yours?" Lev asked, which would have been Evan's next question, too.

"His," Nikki admitted, sitting up and sniffling again, which made her reddened nose scrunch damn cutely. Nik disliked her nose, citing its "flatness," yet Evan had always loved it—the gentle curve of the bridge, and the way it seemed to perfectly match her full lips. As far as he could tell, being with Drew for almost two years hadn't done her any favors in the self-esteem department. Drew was all about improvements and change. Nik had changed plenty in the two years he'd known her, thanks to Drew and his mission to perfect the human physique.

"Do you want to share how he or you define being on different tracks?" Lev, therapist that he was, entered the conversation with a gentle question.

"Not really," Nikki responded. "I'd rather have you be my brother and say Drew is a horse's ass."

Lev smiled, but maintained the therapeutic high ground. In his stead, Evan supplied, "Drew is a horse's ass."

Around the room, heads nodded. Then they all looked at him.

Nikki winced. "I keep forgetting you're his brother. I shouldn't have said that."

"It's all right."

She shook her head. "No, it's not. We had a deal."

"What deal?" Rivka looked between them.

"That we would never compromise our friendship over my relationship with Drew." Nikki gazed at him soberly. "You're not supposed to take sides."

"Actually you said you'd never *ask* me to take sides. And you haven't. I'm offering."

June pressed her hand to the base of her throat. "Oh my gosh, I want a male BFF like you."

"Thanks, hon," Lev deadpanned.

"Well." Rivka sighed heavily. "Forgiveness is a mitzvah, so I'll work on it. But I don't care how far apart the tracks are. Breaking up six weeks before a wedding is *outrageous*. That *shmendrick*. Sorry, Evan."

"It's really, really okay."

June agreed vociferously with her mother-in-law, and they engaged in a discussion about the "right" way to break up.

"What's a *shmendrick*?" Evan asked Nikki beneath his breath.

"It's Yiddish for 'jerk.'"

"Ah." He nodded. "In that case, I agree."

Nikki was wearing one of her ubiquitous sundresses, the flowery, swirly kind she wore even when there wasn't a hint of sun. This one had a black background scattered with yellow, pink and orange flowers.

Five-foot-nothing and so light he bet he could lift her with one arm, she nonetheless gave the impression of being strong, and that wasn't due only to Drew's manic diet and workout routines. Athleticism was a part of her. Long before Drew and his insane workouts, she, Evan and Noah had played copious games of H-O-R-S-E, rode bikes, helped Noah practice T-ball and gone bowling. She liked to move. Liked good food and drink, too, and had…or, rather, used to have…the luscious curves to show for it. Add to that her thick black hair, eyes that were large and nearly black as well, plus skin that was perennially tan, and she looked like someone who belonged on a tropical island. In a bikini, or maybe that was his fantasy life talking. Platonic or not, he noticed her.

"So," he said quietly to Nikki while the others continued to discuss breakup etiquette, "You want to come over later? This afternoon?"

She raised a brow. "Are you trying to find out the ugly details?"

"You don't have to talk about it at all. Although I'd rather hear the details from you than from Drew. If it's any consolation, I doubt he'll give anyone the details. Northrups aren't known for their transparency."

Her eyes darkened to coal black. "Now you tell me."

"Sorry." He didn't point out that she'd never asked. One look at Drew, and she'd fallen. Drew's previous romantic relationships had been deep as a puddle. With Nikki, he'd seemed…better, more attentive, and she'd pulled him into conversations that had gone beyond body mass goals and business models. Some of the time, anyway. The rest of the time she'd been supportive as hell of his brother's limited interests, which had delighted Drew. So, what could Evan have said to persuade his best friend that his brother wasn't good enough for her? Keeping his mouth shut (beyond the initial, admittedly vague cautions) and watching closely had seemed like the best course.

Now he felt guilty as anything, watching Nik's big eyes pool with tears and knowing she'd been excited about every detail of the wedding. Over the past year, she'd texted him from a bridal salon; Crate&Barrel, where they'd registered; taken him to a paper store that printed invitations on recycled paper, which was cool; and had invited him to a cake testing, just the two of them, where they'd debated the merits of white-chocolate, Oregon hazelnut vs. lemon lavender as cake flavors—a conversation she could not have with Drew, who was staunchly antisugar and preferred to "lead by example," even on his wedding day.

Yes, even then he'd kept his big mouth shut.

If anything surprised Evan about Drew bailing on the wedding mere weeks before the event, it was that his brother was more image-conscious than a Kardashian. On the LeanUp With NorthrUp Instagram page, he'd posted the prewedding workout he'd designed for his bride-to-be then crowed that they'd gotten twenty-three thousand views—their highest yet. Nikki, he'd stated proudly, was his good-luck charm. Apparently Drew's ever-increasing fan base loved Nikki's before-and-after photos, along with the fact that Drew had become engaged to a "real woman." (Whom he'd then helped to change, but neither Drew nor his fan base seemed to carry the thought that far.) Evan wondered how his brother would spin the breakup. No matter what, Evan intended to protect Nikki's feelings.

Before he could think too hard about it, the front door opened to admit a flurry of activity in the entryway.

"Hi, everyone! Sorry we're late." Gia Choi, Nikki's youngest sibling bustled into the living room, carrying two shopping bags, each filled to the brim with food, which was like bringing plants to a nursery. Gia's boyfriend, Todd, followed with two additional bags.

"We brought dessert and champagne," Gia announced, raising the bags as she glided into the room. Turning her smile to her sister-in-law, she added, "Nonalcoholic for you. But it's really good. I promise. Mom, it smells crazy delicious in here, as always, and I'm so hungry! We've been shopping all morning—and not just for food! We have news—"

Appearing to realize suddenly that her breezy good cheer was being sucked up in a sea of grim, she looked around. "What? What happened?" She gasped. "Is everyone okay? Where's Dad?"

"Your father's fine," Rivka assured.

"He's out back, playing with Noah," Lev supplied.

Gia's shoulders sagged with relief. "Thank goodness. So what's wrong? You all look…weird." Her perceptive brown eyes zeroed in on the sister that, as far as Evan could tell, she worshipped. Without another moment's hesitation, she rushed to Nikki, sinking to her knees. "You've been crying. What's wrong?"

"I'm okay, Gigi. I'm fine."

"You are not. Mom?"

Evan had commented once on Gia's devotion, prompting Nikki to agree that her sister was an angel, but that she sometimes felt a bit too responsible for Nikki's feelings. When Evan had asked why, Nikki had hesitated. "Gia's a little codependent," she'd said, almost shrugging it off. "I wasn't always the confident, bite-me-if-you-don't-like-me woman you see before you," she'd joked. "In school, I was super sensitive. Gia got used to taking care of my feelings and now it's hard to stop her."

There was more to it; Evan had been certain, but Nikki had moved the conversation along, as she seemed to want to do right now.

"Gia, sweetheart," Rivka said, her tone as heavy as a dirge. "A terrible thing has happened."

"Mom," Nikki protested, tensing beside him.

"What?" Gia's eyes widened in concern. "What terrible thing?"

"Your sister's wedding has been canceled."

"But why?" Gia exclaimed.

"It's okay—" Nikki began, but her mother over-rode. "Drew broke up with her." Grabbing a tissue, Rivka dabbed beneath her eyes. "Six weeks before the wedding, the *farshtinkener*."

"Mom, he isn't—" Nikki began, but was drowned out again, this time by Gia's cry of "He did not!"

Gia proceeded to pepper their mother with questions, which both Rivka and June answered while Nikki turned toward Evan. "He's your brother. You really shouldn't have to listen to this."

He raised a brow. *"Farshtinkener?"*

"Like *shmendrick*, but worse." She reached for his hand. "I don't want this to come between us." Her eyes filled with worry, which yanked his heart out of place.

"Hey, it won't."

Nothing was going to come between him and Nikki. He had no better a track record with women than his relatives. This friendship was the best he'd ever done with a woman and the first stable adult female relationship in Noah's life. Evan relied on Nikki more than she knew. Maybe more than he ought to. He couldn't imagine his life without Nik's rapt way of listening or her laugh, which was inherently joyous and unrestrained.

Leaning over to kiss her temple, he whispered

for her ears only. "Anyone who would hurt you is a *schmendrick farshtinkener.*"

And there it was, mixing with teary relief—a bubble of laughter that made him sure they'd come through this, best friends forever.

Nikki felt Evan's warm breath tickle her ear as he insulted his own brother in clumsy Yiddish. She smelled the mint gum he chewed daily. "My worst vice," he liked to say, which didn't seem bad at all. He was a Wrigley's guy, their Evan. Retro candy and gum were his thing. In the earlier days of their friendship, before she'd met Drew, she'd joined him and Noah on their field trips to Sweet Memories, the coolest candy shop in Holliday, after which they'd tried each other's favorites. Unfortunately, Drew's "health" program that had whittled her down to 14 percent body fat did not allow sugar, retro or otherwise.

"Do you have any Doublemint?" she murmured.

"Yes."

"On you?"

"Yes, again."

She held out her hand, and he began to reach into his pocket, but then she changed her mind. "No, wait. After lunch. Can we eat?" she called out above the voices still raised in ire over the proximity of her dumping to what was supposed to have been her wedding date. She had an ethereal wedding dress, a real beauty, but it would never make it out of her closet now. She intended to eat herself out of the size zero she'd become. "I'm hungry."

At first, she said it only loudly enough for her and maybe Evan to hear. That, however, did not feel nearly big enough.

She was *hungry*, damn it. Practically starving. Working so hard for happiness had been exhausting. Sacrifices had been made—the food she'd wanted to eat, the time and attention Drew couldn't give because he was focused on building his career. She'd been practically starving for the better part of two years.

"I'm HUNGRY!" Nikki hollered above her family's voices, and it felt good.

Everyone was looking at her now.

"Did anyone make challah?"

"Still want gum?"

Seated next beside her at her parents' oval dining table, Evan quirked a thick brown brow at Nikki.

Something minty sounded good, but she was so full of her mother's food and the desserts Gia and Todd had brought that chewing anything, even if she didn't swallow it, felt impossible.

"A stomach pump might be a better after-lunch option at this point."

That elicited a grin from her loyal friend. "'Bout time you ate something more than chicken livers for a meal."

She shrugged. "It was never just chicken livers. We ate grass-fed cow pancreas, too."

"That's truly disgusting."

"I know." She laughed. "Keto was all right, I suppose, but once we went full carnivore…" She shivered. "Blech. I'm really glad to be done with that."

"Are you, though? Truly done with it? You've been 'leaning up' for quite a while. It might not be that easy to let go."

"I know. I think I got addicted to the compliments, all the 'atta girl' moments. And, to the idea that I'd finally 'arrived.' I'm a high school guidance counselor; I should know better, for crying out loud. I *do* know better. But I'm also still the girl who had the biggest thighs in fourth grade. We measured them—can you believe?"

Evan swore softly. "That's brutal."

"Yeah. You think you've done the work to let it go, but…" She shook her head. "When someone shows you how to become exactly what you always thought you should be, it's hard to resist. Although to tell you the truth," Nikki admitted as the conversation swirled around them, "I cheated. A lot. On the diet, and the exercise plan." She leaned close to tell him, "I was supposed to do my age in burpees every day. I never did more than ten at a time. I hate burpees."

The confession and Evan's broad, uncomplicated smile somehow allowed her to shuck off months of feeling guilty or inadequate or whatever the heck she'd been feeling.

"Sometimes I skipped the elliptical and stopped at Dutch Bros for a Golden Eagle Chai. Extra whip," she added in mock horror.

Evan laughed out loud. "I'm glad to hear it. Does Drew know?"

That sobered her. "Yes. Well, not about the burpees—that would have killed him—but he knows I've been eating simple carbs. It's one of the reasons we broke up."

"You're joking."

She shook her head gravely.

That made Evan sober, too. "You realize how insane that is, right?"

He was angry. Nikki gave a half nod, half shrug. Part of her recognized the absolute absurdity of breaking up over a difference of opinion regarding diet. Another part of her realized that fibbing about food was a symptom of something that ran deeper.

"Doesn't matter if it's ridiculous." She patted Evan's sweater-covered forearm. "It's over. For good."

Across the table, Noah stood at Lev's elbow to watch her brother perform a magic trick involving three peas and a cube of tofu. This was what gave her peace: being part of all these sweet connections. Sang was deep in discussion with June. Topic: recipes for the new blender. Rivka, Gia and Todd were extolling the virtues of Fiji.

"When were you in Fiji?" Nikki asked her sister.

"Oh. Um…" Gia exchanged an uncomfortable glance with Todd. "I've never been. I just…think it would be nice."

"Ah. So you want to go and have been doing your usual obsessive research as if this was a thesis project. Todd, a tip about my sister: She is a compulsive planner. You're going to have to take the bull by the horns, bro. Get her to stop planning and *go* somewhere. Have a big adventure."

Another uncomfortable look was exchanged. Couldn't miss it.

"What?" Nikki asked.

"The trip is…uhm…already planned." Gia stammered her response. She poked at the half-eaten truffle on her plate.

"Yeah, it's…planned," Todd agreed with no more conviction than Gia. "Got the plane tickets, and… hotel reservations and…" He trailed off as Gia gave him another furtive glance that made her look more like a spy than a would-be vacationer.

"Okay, you guys. What's the big secret? When you first came in, you said you had news. Is this it— that you're going to Fiji, 'cause that's great! Gigi, I have two amazing bikinis I'm planning to eat my way out of before summer. They'd look terrific on you." Gia never struggled with her weight. Going to the beach or to the neighborhood pool with her had felt like an ordeal when they were younger, because Gia had looked like a teenage Michelle Q, whereas Nikki had carried forty extra pounds on her barely-over-five-foot frame. At whom did guys look? One guess.

Today, following her months of following Drew's dubious plan, Nikki was lean and well-muscled. At first it had been exhilarating to watch her body shed its softness and reveal muscle and strength she hadn't known she possessed. One day she'd found herself staring in the mirror at a woman who had everything she'd ever wanted: an enviable body, a romantic partner who was undeniably hot and successful, a solid career, a closetful of size-nothing clothes. In retrospect, that's when it had all begun to fall apart.

"Do you want my bikinis?" she asked her sister. "I don't need them anymore. I think I may get a dog."

Noah jumped excitedly. "A dog! What kind? My friend Raymond has a beagle and it goes pee on everyone's shoes. Can I walk your dog, Aunt Nikki?"

"Wow, that was a lot to take in. I'm still in the planning stages, kiddo. I have to get the dog first. You could help me decide what kind I want."

"Yes!"

"When did you decide to get a dog?" Rivka asked.

"I like boxers," Sang put in. "Your mother thinks they're too messy, but I would love a boxer."

"They slobber," Rivka said. "It's the jowls."

"What's the correlation between bikinis and dogs?" Evan inquired, curiosity and a hint of amusement in his expression.

"Good question." Gia nodded.

"Out with old, in with the new," Nikki stated. "The bikinis were something I thought I needed, but I'm really more of a cold-weather person. Maybe I'll take up ice skating. Anyway, you'll get way more use out of them in Fiji than I will in the Pacific Northwest. I'm surprised you chose Fiji for a vacay destination," she added. "Last time we talked about travel, you said you were saving Fiji for your honeymoon."

A moment of dead silence was followed by Gia's face turning a deeper shade of red than their mother's candied beets.

"Oh my gosh." Nikki felt her heart skip a few excited beats as, simultaneously, her stomach plummeted. It was an odd feeling. "Did you two finally set a date?" She scrutinized Todd, and sure enough his boy-next-door face gave it away. "You did! You're finally getting hitched! Why didn't you say something?"

"Sweetheart!" Rivka held her hands out to her younger daughter as they all began talking over each other.

"That's why you brought champagne!" Rivka deduced. "Sang, get the flutes so we can celebra— Oh." She stopped abruptly, and suddenly all gazes were on Nikki. "Oh dear."

At first, Nikki wasn't sure what the problem was, but when Gia's eyes teared, her joy swallowed by an exquisite guilt, Nikki understood. Immediately, she knew she had to put a stop to the "Poor Nikki" pity party before it got rolling.

"So when is the wedding date?" she asked brightly. Silence.

Turning toward Evan, she tried to communicate *help out here*, and, bless him, he read her like a book.

"Congratulations, you two. So, Todd, old man, how involved do you want to be in the wedding planning? I mean cake testing is a no-brainer, but are you on board to choose invitations, flowers and all that crap?" Nikki kicked his foot. "All those really fun details?"

The groom-to-be smiled, seemingly relieved to be asked a normal question. "We have started talking about it, actually. We kind of have to if we want to get it done before we move."

"Todd!" Gia exclaimed. Frowning, she gave a suppressive shake of her head.

Todd pushed back. "Gia, we can't just disappear on people. And we don't have a lot of time."

"Disappear? What are you talking about?" Rivka

looked between her youngest child and her fiancé. Receiving no help, she turned to grill her daughter-in-law. "June, do you know anything about this?"

June and Gia were as close as sisters-in-law could be. Glancing nervously at Gia, June stammered, "No?" Rivka lowered her brows, determined to make her sweet daughter-in-law crack. "I mean, I knew Todd was interviewing for jobs out of the country."

Rivka clutched her neck. "What?"

June grimaced apologetically at Gia.

"Sang!" Rivka stared hard at her husband. "Did *you* know about this?" Their father shook his head. Rivka turned her laser-like stare on Nikki. "Did you?"

"First I've heard of it. What kind of job? Which countries? Sounds like a great adventure."

"It sounds like we'll need frequent flyer miles to see our grandchildren."

"Then it'll be an adventure for all of us," Nikki insisted. "We've always said we wanted to travel as a family." Catching the flicker of relief and gratitude that crossed her sister's sweet features—and the horror that flashed across their mother's—Nikki called for reinforcement. "Evan, you worked out of the country for a while, didn't you? You told me it was life-changing."

Shifting toward Rivka, he told her, "I taught English in Monteverde for a couple of years. It was a great experience."

"That's where he met my mom!" Noah pointed out happily enough while he played with the peas and tofu Lev had been using for his magic trick.

For Nikki, any mention of Noah's mother raised discomfort. She knew Evan had been married to Mikaela for four years, that she'd been living in another country most of Noah's life and had no current contact with her son. Questions about the woman tended to dampen the conversation and make Evan moody and closed off, which was not his usual MO, so Nikki had stopped asking. Drew had once supplied the info that Mikaela, Evan's ex, had "a big personality," that Evan had been "obsessed" with the woman and "probably never let her go" despite their being divorced almost since Noah was a baby. Nikki had often wondered if that was the reason Evan couldn't commit to anyone else beyond a few dates.

Noah, for his part, seemed to accept Mikaela's absence, and that had to say something about Evan's ability to navigate rough parenting waters.

"Well," Rivka said, her entire demeanor softened as she gazed at Noah, who was now trying to make the peas disappear into the tofu, "we can travel. And I'm guessing it won't be forever?"

"That's right," Gia confirmed with relief. "Todd's job is in the Netherlands. He was asked to apply for it internally. It's for two years, to get his company's European office up and running, and we'll have a home office I can use and a guest room."

Nikki wanted to hug her sister. Gia was always so eager to placate, too concerned with other people's feelings. "I think it's great," she affirmed. As a copywriter for a large supermarket chain, Gia could live anywhere. "It'll be an incredible adventure."

"When is the move?" asked Sang.

Gia began to look concerned again. Todd took her hand and answered for them. "Two months. We found out about the job a couple of days ago and decided we want to get married before we leave so you all and my family can be there more easily. We thought we'd keep it small and simple—"

"But we're in the talking stages, that's all," Gia cut in, looking helplessly at Nikki. "It's not set in stone, and with the move and being so busy, we…" She raised her brows at Todd in what appeared to be a pleading expression. "We'd probably be better off not attempting an actual wedding right now. Right?"

Todd's expression said that was news to him. "Uhm…well…" His fiancée's panicked expression clearly stopped him from saying more.

Oh, no. No, no, no. Nikki felt inner alarm bells going off. She was not going to be *that* person—the fragile one who was treated as if she could crack at any moment. Nikki was the big sister here, and she intended to act like it.

"Gigi, you've been drawing wedding gowns since fourth grade. You typed a list of possible venues when you were in high school." She turned to her brother-in-law-to-be and grinned. "Sorry if that freaks you out, Todd."

"No, it's cool. I kind of knew."

"Good." Nikki folded her hands on the table and addressed her sister. "A girl who dressed as a bride three Halloweens in a row does not plan a rushed ceremony squeezed in between other people's lavish weddings. Fortunately, I have a much better idea."

Chapter Three

As Gia and the others continued to stare at Nikki wordlessly, she felt Evan's gaze. Great friend that he was, he anted in. "What is your better plan, Nikki?"

"Thank you for asking, Evan. Gia and Todd are going to take Drew's and my venue. She helped me pick it out, anyway." Addressing her sister and future brother-in-law directly, she continued, "You can have the flowers and cake, too. Evan, who has sampled every dessert on the West Coast, says the cake is going to be amazing, but if you don't like the flavors I chose, I'm sure there's time to change. The band is booked, and there's still plenty of time to send out your own invitations. Well, okay, not 'plenty,' but that's what Evites are for. The venue is paid for, so are the cake and flowers, and given how beautifully you wear clothes, you will slay any wedding gown you try on, so get to looking!"

Gia gazed at her in dead silence, her gorgeous amber eyes wide with hope yet cloudy with concern. *Oh boy.* This was going to be a harder sell than anticipated. Nikki glanced around the table. "Am I right, everybody, or am I right?"

Her mother, father and brother appeared traumatized by this idea, and June glanced between her sisters-in-law as if Nikki had just set off an emotional doomsday device. What was wrong with everyone? This was proof, was it not, that she was prepared to move on. Gia deserved a wedding, and hers was up for grabs.

"This is an act of love, people. What's not to like? Evan." She turned toward her friend. "Isn't this a fabulous idea?"

Concern and admiration warred behind his blue eyes. He hesitated.

Oh, no. Et tu, Brute? Being dumped without warning six weeks before the wedding sucked sour pickles, yes. And of course it was cause for extra self-care and lots of snuggles. (Note to self: Start looking on Petfinder.) It was not, however, going to be made any better by her family's worry and pity.

"Evan," she said again, giving him a look at once firm and imploring, "did I ever tell you about the time Gia made me preside over the union of her and her Elmo stuffy when she was four? It was a back-yard wedding. We collected dandelions and daisies for the bouquet and Mom made grilled cheese sandwiches cut into heart shapes for the 'reception.' Gia said it was the happiest day of her life and that she couldn't wait to get married 'for real, to someone who can talk.' When Drew and I got engaged, she dropped everything every time I asked if she could help me with the plans. This wedding is kind of already the wedding of her dreams, too. So, if she takes it for herself and Todd, then I won't have only the memory of a wrecked wedding and a whole lot of forfeited deposits." She switched her focus to Gia alone. "I'll have the memory of my beautiful baby sister and her fella being married in a joyous ceremony and rockin' good party before they move to the Netherlands. Where, I am sure, they will invite me to be their guest for my summer vacation as a gesture of thanks for the small part I played in bringing their wedding to fruition." She placed a hand humbly over her heart. "But really, please, it's not necessary."

Gia laughed through sentimental tears, and Todd looked at his fiancée with anticipation. Rivka and Sang looked proud of Nikki, which lifted her spirits.

Beneath the table, Nikki felt Evan's hand cover hers. He gave her a squeeze. She interpreted that as approval and squeezed his hand in return.

"Okay, then," Nikki said decisively, "it's settled. Are there any truffles left? I'm a little hungry again."

"It was nice of your parents to take Noah to the zoo," Evan commented later that afternoon as he masked off the molding in Nikki's bedroom. Pulling off a long strip of FrogTape, he looked at her dubiously. "I'm sure it wasn't because they'd rather ride the train and watch sea lions than help you paint your entire house. I'm sure this wasn't a well-thought-out plan to sucker me into helping you."

"Absolutely not." Nikki tried to look insulted as she prepared to open a gallon of paint. "This was an entirely *spontaneous* plan to sucker you into helping me paint my entire house."

He shook his handsome head. "At least you're honest."

She smiled as if she didn't have a care in the world at this moment except to pry open the can of paint she'd bought last week when she'd believed Drew would be helping her get her place ready. The intention had been to rent out her house after the school year ended since she would be relocating to Portland to be with him. *That* wasn't happening anymore, yet she still had all this paint she'd bought plus a strong desire to show herself and everyone who'd witnessed her meltdown earlier that she was fine. *Fine.* Not stuck in the past. Rejected, perhaps, but not rejectable. There was a difference. Painting was a good symbolic action.

Before coming over to help her, Evan had gone home to change clothes. They lived a stone's throw from each other on the border between Holliday and the neighboring town of Wurst, where home prices dipped a bit. He'd returned to her place dressed in faded jeans, a pale blue T-shirt he'd tucked in and a Portland Pickles cap that he wore backward. For the record, the casual clothes diminished his physical attractiveness not one jot. Damn the Northrup men and their *GQ* hotness. The admiration of others came too easily to them.

Nikki's baggy boyfriend jeans and even baggier T-shirt did a lot less for her looks than Evan's clothing did for his. The makeup she'd applied so carefully earlier in the day was gone now. The bit left after her crying jag had been scrubbed off once she got home. Now it was just her unadorned face—round regardless of her weight loss, nose too wide and too flat, lips crazy full.

As a high school counselor, she spent a good part of each day telling teenage girls to love and appreciate their uniqueness; as an adult she knew it was easier said than done. Insecurities that took root in childhood tended to grow for years.

"I might not have chosen neutrals if I'd known I was going to live here," she told Evan, changing the channel in her mind, "but I can accent with something bright. Anyway, I think this is a pretty color, don't you?" Using a wooden stir stick, she studied the satin enamel, letting it dribble back into the container in long flat ribbons. "It's called Vanilla Cream. Sounds delicious for a bedroom."

"'Delicious'?" His smile was a little too close to a smirk.

"Yes," she insisted. "I want my bedroom to be a sensuous oasis. Now that I'm staying here, I'm going to get new bedding, too. White with mounds and mounds and mounds of pillows so when I get in bed at night, I'll feel like I'm falling into a bowl of whipped cream."

Evan bungled tearing the tape, which wrapped around his fingers, forcing him to abandon the strip after a few unsuccessful attempts to straighten it out and then shake it off his fingers.

"You're staying at the high school then, right?"

She watched bemusedly as he wrestled another piece of tape. "Yeah. I love it. I was only leaving because Drew is based in Portland. I don't need to leave now. Silver lining," she said brightly.

"Right." Finally managing to release the tape, he knelt and ran a long strip of it along the top of the floor trim. "So, why did you do it?"

"Why'd I do what?"

"Give your wedding to Gia." He moved along the wall, taping as he went. "Seems overly generous under the circumstances. And you didn't just

give it to her, you told her you'd help. I've never pretended to understand why people like weddings in
the first place. They're a money pit with question-
able food, uncomfortable clothes and hyperbolic
speeches everyone's going to regret giving after
they sober up. Okay, Gia wants to get married, you
want to help her, but aren't you turning this into one
of the hardest moments of your life?"

"Listening to what you just said was one of the
hardest moments of my life. Is that what you thought
my wedding was going to be?"

"All except the speeches. *My* best man speech
would not have been hyperbolic."

She shook her head at him. "Weddings are deeply
meaningful, a chance for the couple to celebrate
their happiness with everyone they love."

"And a lot of people they've never met before."

"Pardon me, but weren't you married?"

"Yes, in a rainforest by a Costa Rican lawyer who
happened to be vacationing there with his wife and
son. They were our witnesses. It was spontaneous."

Spontaneous because he was so in love he
couldn't help himself? She was dying to ask but
could already hear the shortness in his tone.

"Are you prepared for questions about you and
Drew?" he continued. "Not to mention how it's
going to feel to smile through every syrupy moment you planned to share with him that now be-
longs to your sister and Todd?"

"Syrupy? I never realized what a curmudgeon you are." He had a point, though. Not about weddings in general, but Gia's in particular. How was it going to feel to watch all those moments Nikki had planned to experience herself? True, Gia had wanted a big wedding since she was a child, but so had Nikki. She had started planning hers at age eight after watching *Father of the Bride*.

Was sudden acute acid reflux a thing? Out of nowhere, she felt indigestion in the extreme.

Summoning every scrap of positivity she possessed, she raised her chin. "You don't put out a fire by running away from it. As far as I'm concerned, it's not my wedding anymore. It's Gia and Todd's. I'm going to help them with it, and I'm going to go and have a wonderful time."

Below his baseball cap, Evan's brows, as attractive a golden-brown shade as his hair, pulled together. "You agreed to be her bridesmaid, Nik. On the same day, in the same place, eating the same food while listening to the same band that was supposed to be yours. You know what that's called?"

"Being a good sister."

"No. People-pleasing. It's called people-pleasing. Or, in some circles, caretaking."

"You don't understand."

"Explain it. You still haven't answered the question: Why?"

Nikki finished stirring, attached a cuff to the

mouth of the can and poured paint into a lined tin, appearing (she hoped) to give it all her concentration, so she didn't have to answer immediately. Okay, maybe repurposing her wedding was a bit over the top. There were things people didn't understand, however. Things Evan didn't understand.

After coating a sponge roller in the paint, she stood and carried the tray to the wall, where she began to apply color in a wide V. With her eyes and hands focused on the task in front of her, she asked, "Do you remember what you said when I told you I was adopted?"

Evan frowned. "No."

"Do you remember the conversation at all?"

Continuing to fit tape against the molding in long, neat strips, he eyed her curiously. "I remember that you were born in Guatemala and adopted at six months."

"Right." It didn't surprise her that he remembered the facts but otherwise hadn't dwelled on the conversation. It was hard for people who grew up with their biological families to understand the way her relationships were nuanced by adoption. "When I told you I was adopted, you said, 'Nice. I have friends who've adopted twice. They're a beautiful family.'"

Pausing in his task, he faced her, genuine puzzlement on his face. "Was there something wrong with or hurtful about that?"

"No! You moved right on to a different topic after that, and I was grateful." Drew hadn't asked many questions, either, save for a few about genetics. Were members of her birth family ectomorphs, mesomorphs or endomorphs, for example, and did she know of any tendencies toward insulin resistance? She'd assumed he'd asked out of professional curiosity.

"I'm always glad when people act as if it's immaterial, simply a fact like having black hair or brown eyes. Except…" Damn, why was it still hard to talk about, after all these years? "It isn't only a fact to me. I struggled with being adopted all through my tweens and teens." She gave him a sideways glance. "I don't have to tell you how intense emotions are during those years."

"Like daily tsunamis in middle school."

"Hourly."

With a huff of laughter, he nodded. Working in schools gave them a common ground.

"Well, it all got pretty dark for me during eighth grade and my freshman year of high school," she admitted. "Lots of depression and anxiety. I felt disconnected from everyone, including myself."

She had all Evan's attention. "Why?"

"You're big on *Why?* today." Even after all these years, the old, old feeling of isolation and desperation remained within arm's reach. Merely thinking of that time in her life clogged her throat again now, as if she were still fourteen. Trying to keep the moment as light as possible, she shrugged. "How many middle schoolers do you know who want to stick out like a sore thumb? Even emo kids have a group. It has to do with mirror neurons, right? Most everyone wants to belong to something. When I was in school, the only other adopted kid was blonde and blue-eyed, like her family." Maybe that was enough said for now. "The point is, it scared my family quite a bit, especially Mom and Gia."

Evan's expression was calm but confused. "We've been friends two years. You've never mentioned struggling with any of this before."

"No." Recalling that time in her life could still fill her with guilt. Pausing to reload the roller, she stared at the paint tray before glancing back to Evan, who looked almost…hurt. "Hey, big guy," she teased, "you don't talk about your ex-wife, either. Don't think I haven't noticed. And I don't push it, in case you haven't noticed."

"No, I've noticed."

"Part of our charm is the way we respect each other's boundaries. That's a major reason we feel so comfortable together."

Beneath the backward Pickles cap, Evan's smile twisted into something wry. "I imagine you're right."

Nodding, she started on the wall again. "Of

course, I am. There's no angst. How many relationships can you say that about?"

He tipped his head in acknowledgment. "Not many." He returned to taping.

Nikki nodded, pleased until the conversation failed to pick up again, which was unlike them. Before she could think of a topic, the doorbell rang.

"Hopefully that's someone with a strong desire to paint your living room," he cracked as she rose.

"Ha ha." Leaving him in the bedroom, she went to answer the front door.

It was not someone who wanted to paint. It was Gia, who lived over an hour away, standing alone on her doorstep.

"Hey, this a surprise! I get to see you twice in one day?" Nikki exclaimed. "Come in."

"Thanks." Gia crossed the threshold, clutching her purse and hunching her shoulders as if she was cold even though it was an unseasonably warm spring day. "Sorry to just drop in. I was upset and went for a drive to think, and I just kept driving and thinking until I wound up here."

One look at Gia's red-rimmed eyes filled Nikki with concern. She pulled her sister into the living room and guided her to the couch. "Do you want coffee? Tea?" When Gia shook her head to both, Nikki sat beside her sister and said, "What's wrong, sweetie?"

Her beautiful eyes filled with tears. "I'm a horrible sister!"

"Gigi. What are you talking about? You're the best sister ever. Where is this coming from, honey?"

"You gave me your wedding. *Your* wedding." Gia flopped her free hand. "And I accepted! What kind of selfish sister does that? I asked you to be my maid of honor. I suck!"

"No, you do not suck."

"But Nikki, I *can't* take your *wedding.*"

As her heart thumped, Nikki attempted to nip that thinking in the bud. Taking Gia's free hand and holding on firmly, she said, "Listen to me. You are a wonderful sister and always have been. The best. C'mon, you sneaked your cookies into my lunch every day before we left for school, even though you lived for Nutter Butters. Remember when I was twelve and Mom and Dad had to cancel my birthday figure skating party because I broke my leg? We each got a party every other year, and you said you didn't want a party that year so I could have yours."

Gia gave a sniffly laugh. "I knew how much you loved birthdays."

"Yes, I did. But so did you. As unselfish as it was to give me your birthday party, you did it for the wrong reasons." Because it appeared Gia was about to disagree, Nikki doubled down. "You need to stop...compensating for me. I don't want it."

"Compensating for you? I've never done that.

I'm not even sure what you mean. I just don't want to suck as a sister."

Perhaps it was time to talk about the past, after all, because the pattern of little sister rescuing big sister needed to stop. "Eighth grade. Livvi Beattie. Remember? I came home from school and climbed up to our tree house because Incredibly Loud Livvi asked me in front of the entire class why my 'real' parents didn't want me. I knew the truth. I'd heard it all my life: My birth mother couldn't take care of me because she made three dollars a week and had three other children under six... Mom had prayed and prayed for a child and the moment she saw me she knew that I was her daughter... She carried me in her heart instead of under it... I'd heard those things all my life, but none of it mattered in the moment. Having a classmate ask why my 'real' parents didn't 'want' me and watching all the other kids look at me like they'd been wondering the same thing for years—it changed things. I didn't want it to, but it did."

Nikki tried to speak as matter-of-factly as she could even though the sting never quite left. "I went up to our tree house and stayed there, crying, for two hours until you came up to tell me Mom wanted us to come in for dinner, and I got super dramatic and said I was never going to school again or leaving the tree house even if they chopped it down, and I wasn't a real Choi, anyway, so I didn't have to go in to dinner. You started crying, too, but then you climbed down and begged Mom to let us have a sisters' sleepover up there and offered to forfeit play dates for the rest of the school year if she said yes. Then you climbed back up with dinner and blankets, and the next day you started slipping me your cookies and telling everyone at your school that you wished you'd been adopted, because several scientific studies showed that adults who'd been adopted as children had better careers, traveled more and lived in much nicer homes than people who hadn't been adopted. Most of Duniway Elementary needed therapy by the time you got done with them."

Gia had been listening with a frown on her perfect brows. Now she offered a sheepish shrug. "Incredibly, Loud Livvi's brother was in my class. I thought it might get back to her."

"It did." Nikki squeezed her sister's arm. "It was a rock star sister move, Gi. And I appreciate the motivation behind it to this day. But you've been apologizing for being a birth child ever since." Before Gigi could utter the denial she was already forming, Nikki pointed out, "You and Todd have been engaged a *lot* longer than Drew and I. You didn't wear your engagement ring until after I had one. Why?"

"I wore it…places," she stammered. "It was at the jewelers."

"For eleven months?"

"I'm difficult to size."

"Mm. You feel sorry for me."

"No, I don't! I love you."

"I know. It doesn't change the fact that ever since my meltdown in the tree house, you've seen me as someone who needs to be treated with kid gloves."

"It wasn't just the tree house."

Nikki knew exactly what her sister meant. She could see the guilt Gia felt for referencing a past her family rarely talked about. "Okay." She nodded, holding her sister's hand even more tightly. "I can't imagine how scary it was for you to see me the way I was back then. Depression frightened the hell out of me, too. When I see photos of myself during that time—" She shook her head. "I looked like I didn't want to be here."

Gia nodded, her eyes filling with tears after all these years.

"I'm sorry, Gigi." And then she remembered something. "I got really thin back then, didn't I?"

"You were skin and bones. You never wanted to eat."

"Depression does that. And you were always bringing me food." Nikki shook her head. She'd been a dunce. "Did my getting thin again trigger you?"

The question surprised Gia at first, but then she thought about it. "Maybe it did. I have been worried about you. I mean, you look amazing—strong this time—but…it bothered me that Drew was so proud of you for losing weight."

"Yeah." Maybe that should have bothered her, too. She'd wanted it so much for herself that she'd focused on the endless praise he'd given her and ignored the raised brow when she'd suggested a cheat day. "I get that. If it's any consolation, I'm reevaluating what it means to be fit. And what it means to have self-esteem. I just really wanted a bikini body for once in my life."

"Bikinis come in lots of sizes."

Said the girl with the tush you could bounce a quarter off. But Nikki knew Gia would say she was beautiful—and mean it—no matter what size Nikki was. And that was pretty nice thing to know.

"Let me give you this wedding, will you? Let me be the big sister. It will make me feel better, much. Like I'm a warrior, not a victim of circumstance. It'll reassure Mom and Dad, too," she added, bringing out the heavy artillery. "They've been dying to see one of us get married, and at this point a trip up the aisle sounds as appealing to me as a case of chicken pox."

"Oh, Nik…"

"I'm not saying I'll feel that way forever. Right now I want to focus on myself, have some fun. Eat my weight in Swiss meringue buttercream." She looked at her sister cajolingly. "So are we gonna eat some wedding cake?"

Gia was tempted, Nikki could tell, but not yet

convinced. "Todd and I don't need a big wedding. We'd be happy with something in the backyard or at the justice of the peace."

"Todd might be, but you wouldn't. Can you honestly see yourself getting married downtown by a justice of the peace in a bad suit and toasting each other with paper cups?"

"They let you bring sparkling cider."

"It's not your dream."

"People grow up. Their dreams change."

"You don't buy wedding magazines anymore? You don't have subscriptions to *Bridal Guide*, *The Knot* and *Martha Stewart Weddings*? You don't want to be married under a *chuppa*?"

She was weakening. Nikki could tell. Still, Gia exclaimed, "This cannot be easy for you. Why are you acting like it's easy?"

"I didn't say it was easy."

"Aha!" Gia stabbed a finger at her. "I knew it. I told Todd it would be too painful for you to do this after something as traumatic as being left practically at the altar—"

"Hey, beautiful, I'm going to take a shower. Mind if I use the towel on the door— Oh. Hey, Gia."

Both women turned toward the silky baritone. Nikki wasn't sure who was more surprised, her or Gia as Evan walked in from the bedroom with his shirt off...like *off* off...his jeans resting low on his hips and his feet bare when only moments before he'd been wearing a pair of running shoes. He looked at Nikki as if he was a lion and she was a steak he'd like to lick all over before devouring it.

"Hi... Evan?" Gia answered, looking almost as confused as Nikki felt. Gia glanced at her sister with her jaw slack. "Uhm... I'm sorry, I didn't realize..."

As Nikki was about to claim there was nothing to realize, Evan strolled to her side, put his arm around the back of her waist and pressed a tiny, provocative kiss to her temple. "May as well tell her."

Nikki turned her head, looking up, probably a mistake with his mouth mere inches away. Her brain was pure static. No rational thought seemed to be able to make it through.

"Ohhhh," Gia breathed. "Is this why you and Drew..."

"No! Lord, no." Gesturing to Evan, Nikki sputtered, "This is not what you think. This is—"

She had no clue what this was.

Evan was no help, gazing at Gia with a crooked smile. "Nothing happened while Nikki was with Drew. I promise I'm not that guy. But today at lunch I knew I had to say something before I lost her to someone else. Again." He turned back to Nikki. "I've waited a long time to tell this one how I feel. I wasn't sure I'd ever get the chance."

What the hell? He sounded like the end of a rom-com.

With a mix of surprise and flagrant delight, Gia

WENDY WARREN 69

put her hands over her mouth as she squealed then started to clap. "This is *so* romantic. Wait… Today? It just started today? And you've already— Wow. Good for you. Why waste time? I mean, we've always talked about how you two were perfect for each other."

Nikki began to fully appreciate the expression *my head is spinning*. "We?"

Gia nodded. "June and I. And Lev. And cousin Shira the first time Drew and Evan came to Passover—but just that once. After that she never mentioned how much better you and Evan would be together than you and Drew. It's not that we didn't like Drew," she hastened to assure. "It's just that you and Evan have so much in common, and you guys have always had that sexy best friend vibe. Do you think this was meant to be? That Drew was kind of a placeholder until you were both ready? Again, no offense to Drew."

Gia obviously wanted one of them to say, *Yes, this was definitely meant to be*.

When Nikki hesitated, Gia's brow pinched in concern. "Is this a rebound thing?" She covered her mouth again. "Darn it! That slipped out. Sorry, Evan."

"Not to worry, Gia. We're still in the exploration phase. Right, Snoopy?"

"Snoopy?" Gia giggled. "That's so cute."

Evan nodded. "I've always teased Nik that she

looks like Snoopy when she's happy. And she calls me Charlie Brown." He pulled her closer, giving her waist a squeeze. "Don't you, Snoop?"

Like that would ever happen.

Gia's cupid's bow lips spread into a wide, delighted grin.

"No," Nikki contradicted, but forced a wide, toothy smile. "I'm not calling you that. Not in public, anyway." Reaching around Evan's back, she pinched his arm as hard as she could. Talk about using a cannon to swat a fly.

"I can't believe how cute you two are." Gia squealed with excitement. "Who else knows about this? Oh, no one, right? Because you only just did…" She raised her brows and nodded. "Got it."

No, she did not "got it." Gia thought they'd just had sex.

"This is not what you're imagining. We were in there—" she gestured toward her bedroom "—opening paint."

"Paint? Like to roll around in or something?" Gia asked.

"Oh my Lord. No. Gia!" She glared at Evan, who was trying not to laugh. *Look what you started.* Obviously Evan thought he was helping her—in some bizarre way—but she was going to tell her sister the truth. "This is incredibly awkward."

"What she means," he interrupted, "is that the physical part of our relationship is just getting started. It's new. We're working out the kinks, but I think from what we've experienced so far it's safe to say we're headed in the right direction."

"Oh my gosh, you guys, of course. It doesn't always work right away. This isn't *Masters of Sex*. Todd and I took a while to get in the groove, too." She nodded confidentially. "There's nothing to be ashamed of. It's like I told him, there are prime-time commercials now about premature ejaculation and tons of ways to work on it—"

"Gia, Gia, Gia!" Nikki shook her head. She could feel Evan shaking with mirth beside her.

"TMI? Okay, but you know what I mean."

"Absolutely." Evan bounced Nikki in a side hug. "It's bound to get better. Someday, this one and I... We're going to put the *whoop* in whoopie."

"Oh my gosh, you are so darling!"

Whipping out her cell phone, Gia took a photo of them and immediately started editing. "I'll send this to you."

"Great. Thanks." Nikki put her hand on Evan's chest. She could feel the thump of his heart beneath her palm. Smiling in her sister's direction while Gia appeared to text someone, she grabbed a few of Evan's chest hairs between her thumb and index finger and tugged as hard as she could.

Nearly stumbling forward, he grunted with pain then captured her hand in his. "Chill on the sadistic tendencies, would you, Snoopy?" he growled softly.

"You are crazy, you know that?" she uttered just as quietly through clenched teeth. "What are you thinking?"

"Do you mind if I tell June?" Gia asked. "I know it's your news, and if you'd rather tell everyone yourselves, I completely understand. But June was so worried about you having a birthday right after breaking up." She shook her head. "That would have been torture."

"My birthday isn't for weeks."

"I know, but…" Her smile was joyous. "It'll be so much better spending it with Evan. So, can I? Tell everyone?"

Caught in the lie's web already. Damned if she did and damned if she didn't. Telling the truth now would be cruel. Gia would feel like an idiot. Besides, it would set her up for weeks of anxiety, maybe *months* with wedding season upon them.

Evan had handed her a solution to her family's worry in general and to Gia's guilt over the wedding in particular, but at what price?

Gia waited for an answer. "Sure," Nikki decided, nodded gamely at her sister, "go ahead. *Have at it.*"

"June is going to flip. I'll call her." Walking a few paces away, Gia tapped her phone screen.

"You better have a plan beyond this moment," Nikki whispered fervently to Evan, "because in about five minutes, my entire family is going to believe we're sleeping together."

He nodded. "We have a few options," he murmured back.

"What are they?"

"I can say I was kidding. But that would make me look weird, and I have an image to uphold."

"Option two?"

"You could wait a few days, then tell your family you realized you're just not that into me."

"And make them worry even more, because now they think I'm rash and erratic? Next option."

"We let it ride. And, we bear in mind that we told only a partial lie."

"How do you figure?"

With her still glued to his side for Gia's sake, Evan glanced down at her. "It pains me that you have to ask."

"What?"

He shook his head. "That forgettable, was it? I'm referring to the fact that we did sleep together. Once." Lowering his head, he added even more softly, "And speaking for myself, I thought we were damn successful at putting the *whoop* in whoopie."

Chapter Four

"So your sister and her fiancé and your brother and his wife and your mother and father all think you're sleeping with your recently ex-fiance's half-brother?"

Eden Berman-Soon-To-Be-Bowen, Nikki's best friend since college, wrapped newspaper around a coffee mug and packed it into a box with other mugs, cups and saucers. Standing on one side of the small kitchen peninsula in the beloved duplex she was preparing to vacate, Eden looked somewhat entertained. She'd expressed support after Nikki announced her breakup with Drew, although the tenor of that support had been less "Aw, sweetie, I'm so sorry" and more "Drew is the asshat of the decade."

"Right," she answered Eden.

"And how do the Chois feel about this development?"

"*Pretend* development," Nikki reminded. "My mother called to tell me that she and my dad love Evan so if I'm happy, they're happy, and I shouldn't worry at all about what people will say because what happens on *Bachelor in Paradise* is way, way worse."

Eden laughed. "She's right."

"And Gia and June are thrilled, which is a little insulting since they were about to be my bridesmaids."

Eden moved cups around in the box, making more room. Her silence spoke volumes.

"I know how you felt about Drew," Nikki acknowledged. "I realize he sometimes came across as a bit superficial."

"He looked like his muscles were carved from Carrara marble, and he wanted you to look that way, too."

Eden had spent many years coming to terms with a body that had been injured in a car accident when she was a teen. It hadn't been easy to accept her scars, but she'd done it. The push for physical perfection was not something that sat well with her.

"Drew isn't an overly complicated person," Nikki said in an understatement. Her ex-fiancé was more comfortable with the external world than the internal one. He'd called Nikki his muse and had wanted her to be his partner in business as well as in life. LeanUp With NorthrUp was poised to go national and would need a senior staff counselor to promote healthy minds along with healthy bodies. Nikki had liked the idea. Becoming lean and fit for the first time in her life had felt powerful. Euphoric. She had been strong, sexy and engaged to a man with five million YouTube subscribers...yes, she'd enjoyed it.

Now that it was over, she needed some time to lick her wounds and figure out what she wanted at almost thirty-seven years old. Maybe she'd finish out her school year and go on a long summer vacation. Alone.

Wrapping the Help Wanted ads around a mug that read, Today's Excellent Attitude Is Sponsored by Coffee, Nikki commented, "I should let my family deal with their own anxieties about my being single while I handle mine."

"But?"

"That would be very out of character for me."

"Right." Eden nodded sagely. "No point in pretending you're not going to be at least a little codependent about this."

"Or a lot. When I got depressed in eighth grade, I filled journals with writing that could make Sylvia Plath seem bubbly. It worried my mother sick. She was diagnosed with her first bout of breast cancer the very next year, and I blamed myself for causing her so much stress."

Eden stopped what she was doing and said soberly, "It takes ten years for a breast tumor to grow before it's detected."

Nikki sighed. "I know. But it can take a lifetime to let go of beliefs we form during a period of trauma. I'm still working on it." After nestling the mug in the box they were loading, she picked up a small glass coffee press Eden had set out and began to wrap it. "My mom had another breast tumor removed two years ago—did I tell you that? She's fine, but no way am I going to risk causing her more grief. I'm not capable of that kind of detachment."

"Well, you're a good daughter."

"I'm realistic. Gia's wedding is going to take her mind off my breakup. Especially if I can convince them that I am perfectly fine with the way things are turning out."

"Enter the hot affair with your ex-fiancé's brother."

Groaning, Nikki shook her head. "No, that was not my plan! It's a complication. Honestly, I wanted to strangle Evan when he said it, but I also understand why he did. He thought he was helping."

"Maybe it will be a help. I know it's not completely above board, but at Gia's wedding either people are going to tell you how awful they feel because your fiancé left you or they'll whisper about how quickly you bounced back. Pretending you and Evan are more than friends seems like a pretty decent solution. It's temporary and you don't have to go Instagram public. You can contain it. Also, not that I'm shallow as a puddle or anything, but before Gia's wedding, you're going to my brother's. And then in the summer you're my maid of honor. Attending without a plus one under the circumstances?" She wagged her head. "Very bad idea. Going with a hot guy?" She pointed her index finger at Nikki and winked. "Much better. Instead of asking you a lot of undesirable questions, people will gossip about you in the bathroom."

"Awesome."

Leaving the packing, Nikki crossed to the counter where she'd deposited the snack bags she'd brought for them and ripped open the nacho-flavored roasted kale, about to take a bite when Eden's rambunctious snow-white cat, Malfoy, jumped onto the counter beside her and released one of his demanding, piercingly loud yowls.

"Sorry!" Eden grimaced. "With all the moving, he's been extra hungry."

"Extra hungry? As long as you've had this cat he's eaten enough to put weight on a Great Dane." Abandoning the kale for the moment, Nikki opened a package of Babybel and let Malfoy attack the small wheel of cheese.

Bringing the kale chips back to Eden and offering her some before taking a handful for herself,

Nikki said, "It's still weird, this idea of pretending to date Evan. What are the Northrups going to think? It can't be good for Evan's relationship with his family."

"No, but Evan is a big boy, and he must be okay with it. From what you've shared, the Northrups have plenty of their own issues to worry about. Besides, you and Evan had a relationship before you ever met Drew. Frankly, given that Drew has an ego the size of Mount Hood—I feel I can say that now since you two are over—I'm surprised it didn't drive him crazy when you told him you and his brother once slept together."

Nikki shoved a huge wad of kale chips in her mouth and began crunching.

Eden peered at her. "You did eventually tell Drew about the night you spent with Evan?"

"Mmbubhmbubnut."

Eden's eyes got huge. "You said you were going to tell him."

Swallowing with difficulty, Nikki countered, "I said I was going to tell him *if* it seemed like the right thing to do. It never did." To Eden's doubtful expression, she reminded, "I hadn't even met Drew when Evan and I—" She circled her hand.

"Slept together."

"Once! Only once. He and I had agreed we were not going to talk about that night. That part of our relationship was over practically before it began."

"Yes. I'm sorry, why was that again?"

"Because we both realized we were better off as friends."

"Yet the sex was good. You said the sex was good. Am I remembering that correctly?"

"It was fine. Do you have green tea?"

Eden waved a hand toward the kitchen. "In my tea drawer. So, was it only 'fine'? You were always a little vague about that."

Nikki got up to look in Eden's tea drawer, which was crammed with boxes of green and herbal teas. She felt her friend's gaze like the heat of a burning sun. "Maybe I was a little vague, because the sex was a little vague."

Darn. Now she was lying to her best friend about her other best friend. "I'm not saying he wasn't good in bed. I'm saying that maybe the sex part of the evening is vague, because it never should have happened in the first place. So I can't recall it. In detail."

Although she could.

Recall it.

In detail.

Sex with Evan had put the *whoop!* in whoopie. Desperate to change the subject, she pulled a box from the drawer and read the label. "What's Clarity Tea?"

"It has herbs that contribute to mental sharpness." Meaningfully, Eden arched a well-shaped brow. "Keeps your memories from becoming too vague."

"You're a hoot."

Eden shrugged. "Well, I guess telling Drew is a moot point now."

"I'd say so."

"Any chance you and Evan might reprise the... vagueness?"

"No." Grabbing two bags of organic green tea, Nikki filled a pot with water. "No chance."

"I don't get it." After picking her way through the box-filled room, Eden opened a cooler, pulled out a jar of local Busy Bee honey and brought it to the kitchen. "There must have been some spark there. And you two seem so right together. You're both in education, you laugh at each other's jokes and you spend more time with him than you did with Drew."

"Drew traveled for work."

"Plus," Eden continued as if Nikki hadn't spoken, "you want a family, and Evan has a proven track record for making great kids."

Nikki felt a dull throb behind her eyes and wondered whether Eden had already packed the Tylenol. "I expected this from my family, not from my best friend—the one who avoided romance for ten years before she met her fiancé."

"Exactly. Last man on Earth I thought I'd go for, but here I am, happier than I ever thought I could be."

Nikki would have to be the most churlish person on the planet to begrudge her friend such joy.

Her own story was going to play out differently, however.

"Why not keep an open mind about Evan?" Eden suggested. "What could it hurt? Nothing ventured, nothing gained. Right? You never know, you could wind up—"

"He's still in love with his ex-wife."

That information proved to be a very effective conversation stopper.

"I think," she added to be fair.

Eden stared at her. "You think."

Nikki sighed. "He's never said so directly. Evan is a cynic when it comes to weddings, but last year when the middle school band teacher and the high school drama teacher got engaged, we were both invited to the party, which was at a microbrewery. Everyone was making toasts and then Evan stood up and said he wished the couple a long marriage, because being married to your soul mate is one of the greatest gifts life can bestow."

"Oh. Okay, but he's not married anymore."

"No." When she'd met Drew—while they had been trainer and trainee, not yet dating—he'd offered up the information that Evan still loved Mikaela, a fact which Drew had found somewhat pathetic, apparently, as his opinion had been that Mikaela was "a lost cause" as a wife and mother. "My brother," Drew had said, "loves a lost cause."

"Evan never wants to date anyone more than a

few times. I don't think he wants to be married again. He hasn't moved past that time in his life, and I don't want to play around. He's no more interested in a romance with me than I am with him. We're friends. No benefits. Just friends. And we're going to keep it that way."

Eden nodded slowly. "All right, I get it. At least you each have a plus-one when you need it. That's a benefit right there."

"Yeah. Yeah it is."

Evan had commissioned the art instructor at his middle school to paint a mural on one of the walls in Noah's bedroom. The color-saturated, life-size canvas depicted a scene in which the characters from his son's favorite books—and also from a few of Evan's—converged to trek through a jungle, discover treasure at the bottom of the ocean and stand on the top of a mountain to gaze at the stars.

Before he'd become a father, Evan had speckled his own life with adventure. Winter and summer vacations had been for traveling. He'd ridden a motorcycle across the US, backpacked in Ireland, climbed Iceland's Hvannadalshnúkur in a fifteen-hour straight shot. Neither pain, fatigue nor anxiety had ever intimidated him. Very little had intimidated him.

Until Noah.

Only parenting could bring Evan Northrup to his knees.

"Talia Decker should not have said what she did," Evan told his son as he sat beside Noah on the twin "big boy" bed they'd picked out together for Noah's fifth birthday. He was six now and asking more questions than ever before. "It was unkind and untrue."

"But she *did* say it, Dad!" Noah complained pragmatically. "She said Special Person's Day isn't for special persons. Teachers just call it that so the kids whose mothers don't love them won't feel bad."

It had to be wrong to dislike a fellow six-year-old in his son's first-grade class, but in that moment Evan felt it. Intense. Dislike.

One of the unexpected realities of parenting was that when his kid felt pain, Evan felt it ten times harder. He'd just had his heart cut out with a spoon and served to him by Talia Decker, who had two parents, including a mother who was the president of the PTA and room mom for Ms. Cheney's classroom of twenty-seven six-year-olds.

"Everybody on the bus heard her and no one said it wasn't true." Noah's heavy brows, characteristic of Northrup males, were drawn together in a frown that would have been adorable if he hadn't felt legitimately wounded.

"No one said it wasn't true, because no one was listening to Talia." What Evan's response lacked in community spirit, he hoped it made up for in conviction. "What were Luca and Zak doing while Talia was talking?" Noah shrugged. "Paying no attention to her, I bet. Was Luca talking about his Hot Wheels collection?"

"Yes."

"Exactly. And Zak was wondering how to convince his parents to get him a Robo Alive Dragon Ice. He wasn't listening to Talia, either."

Noah looked as if he was being persuaded, but then he said, "I want Aunt Nikki." His expression was firm and belligerent.

The fact that it was eight o'clock at night with school the next day notwithstanding, Evan knew Nikki was uncomfortable as hell with him at the moment. They hadn't spoken since yesterday after he'd suggested to Gia that they were starting a relationship.

And, yeah, he'd implied they had slept together last Saturday, but he'd had to think on his feet, and he was a guy.

Nik had been adamant that he'd started more fires than he'd put out. He disagreed. Her family liked him; this was an excellent solution. *You're welcome.*

Their friendship had never gone through a silent period before, and it was unsettling. Even after they'd had sex for real a couple years ago, and she'd made it crystal clear it was one night only, they'd carried on as usual.

The very next day, she'd called and invited him and Noah over to make peanut butter–butterscotch Rice Krispies Treats and to play Scotland Yard Junior. Back to their regularly scheduled programming. And he'd been grateful.

He should have been grateful.

He hadn't been in the market for a relationship back then, certainly not with someone whose feelings he would have to tend. And that's the way it would have been with Nikki, because they'd already been on the road toward best friendship. Evan had known he would start feeling responsible for her—for her feelings, for her happiness. He hadn't had the emotional bandwidth for that.

Which was why, when she had calmly and reasonably (one could say almost dispassionately) insisted that their single night of sex would remain exactly that—one night only and just sex—he'd been appreciative.

Hundred percent.

"It's too late to call Aunt Nikki tonight—" he began.

"No, it's not. Gimme your phone. I'll text her."

"Okay first, what happened to *please*?"

"Please, can I text her?"

"And second, you know there's no electronics at bedtime." Refraining from mentioning that his son didn't know how to spell well enough to text some-one, Evan motioned for Noah to scooch beneath the covers. "Anyway, I know what Aunt Nikki would tell you."

"What?"

"She'd say, *Noah, you're the coolest kid ever. A million and thirty-five people love you today.*"

Noah smiled, showing the pretty-damn-cute gap where his front teeth used to be. "How does Aunt Nikki know it's that many?"

This was a game Evan had watched Nikki play with Noah dozens of times.

"A million and twelve people love you today, Noah Boah."

"How do you know?"

"I counted. It took a long time. I was late for work."

Pulling Noah's blanket over his shoulders, Evan leaned forward to kiss his son on the cheek and to whisper in his ear, "She counted. And I double-checked. It was a million thirty-five on the nose." Pulling back a few inches, he added, "Go to sleep in fifteen minutes, and we'll call Aunt Nikki in the morning, before school. Deal?"

"Deal." Noah snuggled down. "I'm going to ask her to come to Special Person's Day."

Evan's chest pinched. He'd assumed he'd be going as the "special person" by default. Touched that Nikki had such an impact on his son, he said,

"She'll like that you asked her." And, if he knew Nik, she'd use her paid time off to make sure she could go.

"Okay, tell me something you're grateful for." It was part of their final nighttime ritual, after which Noah was virtually guaranteed to start yawning if he hadn't already.

"I'm grateful Talia Decker doesn't sit next to me in class."

Not exactly the positive appreciation Evan had in mind, but fair enough.

"Tell me something you hope for."

"I hope Talia Decker *never* sits next to me in class."

Evan couldn't help it: he laughed loudly. "Predictable, dude." Pulling the covers down, he blew a quick raspberry on Noah's tummy then tucked him in again. "All right, last one: Tell me something you like about you."

"I liiiike…being funny!"

"You are that."

Rolling onto his side, Noah burrowed deeper under the covers. "I'm going to dream about Disneyland."

"Good plan." Evan gave his son a final goodnight kiss, watched the first yawn claim him and turned off the bedside lamp.

"Night, Dad."

"Night, my son."

Walking down the hall to the living room of the three-bedroom bungalow Evan had purchased on a sweet lot at the southernmost edge of Holliday, he felt the familiar weight of parenting on his own. *Am I screwing this up? Will my kid be scarred for life? Was I more arrogant than optimistic to think we'd be okay?*

Damn it, Mikaela.

Five years, four months. That's how long she'd been gone. That's how long he'd been hoping she'd return, so he wouldn't have to explain to his son— their son—why she'd left in the first place.

By the time he reached his living room, Evan was doing what he'd promised himself he would not do again.

Grabbing his cell phone from the coffee table, he said, "Call Mikaela."

Realizing Noah might not be fully asleep yet and unwilling to risk his overhearing the conversation, Evan opened the front door and stepped onto his porch, the phone pressed to his ear. It rang only once.

"The number you have dialed is no longer in service. Please check the number and dial again."

A brief pause followed before the message began to repeat. He didn't listen to it a second time. Swearing coarsely, he disconnected, barely resisting the urge to smash the phone against the porch pillar.

She'd promised. Mikaela had *promised* him she

would make sure he always had her contact info. Once before, two years ago, she'd changed numbers—and countries, moving from El Salvador back to Costa Rica—without telling him for ten months. Quite likely, that's what was happening now—another move, another important project, another time when the promise that Evan would always be able to get in touch in an emergency became little more than an afterthought in her feverish, chaotic, mission-driven life. She'd get around to telling him eventually. What difference did it make, really? She'd never desired contact with him or Noah, either regular or sporadic.

Breathing as deeply as he could, Evan filled his lungs with the clean, sweet night air in the small town that would make Mikaela roll her eyes if she ever visited. So much privilege here, the people fed and happy and employed, baskets of flowers hanging from the streetlamps, lights sparkling from sundown to sunup. She wouldn't see the care, planning and hopefulness that contributed to the small, admittedly touristy, unabashedly comfortable community. To Mikaela, Evan's move here would be baffling at best; at worst, it would signify a return to the bloated, acquisition-driven lifestyles of their respective parents. A mutual disgust for that world had drawn him and Mikaela together in the first place. As she'd pointed out the day she'd told him she was pregnant, her attitude and her goals had never changed from the day they'd first met.

It was hard to practice a bloated lifestyle on a teacher's salary, and few people in Holliday—except for the town's namesake, the Hollidays themselves—were financially wealthy. Evan had accepted a job here as a single father, because it felt damn good to walk down streets where people knew your kid and cared about him. Not because of who *you* were, but because of who *they* were: damn fine people.

The woman he'd married would not see it that way. With every Victorian-garbed caroler who stood in front of a house in winter and every firework that glittered in the sky on the Fourth of July, she would see excess, not community spirit and the desire for a simpler, kinder life. She would feel her own life closing, not opening.

Moot point anyway. It wouldn't matter where Evan lived. Choosing fatherhood had ended his marriage.

Expecting someone to be different from who they were was a recipe for anger and resentment. Expecting what you couldn't have? Useless, misery-making futility.

Another deep breath returned him to acceptance, even if it was an awkward, ungraceful version of acceptance.

The truth was, he was lucky. Noah was lucky. Evan's family, while not the warmest socks in the dryer, were, nevertheless, present and willing to be involved…in their Victorian-drawing-room, we-wish-children's-hands-weren't-so-sticky way. Better still, his neighbors in Holliday lobbied for the privilege of babysitting or building Noah's new bike or teaching him to bake a bread.

Also, there was, he believed, one person in this great big world who had quickly come to love his son as wholly and as unselfishly as Evan did. Feeling a need that was stronger than any of his reservations, he decided to go ahead and text her:

Can you talk?

Then he leaned against the porch railing and waited.

Chapter Five

Nikki brought a bottle of Evan's favorite brandy over to his place. She wasn't having any, and he'd poured himself only a splash given that it was a school night and he was the sole caretaker of his six-year-old son. Still, Nikki was glad she'd brought it. A bottle of Chatelle Napoleon V.S.O.P. said "Truce."

Sitting on his couch, speaking softly so Noah wouldn't wake up, Nikki answered the question Evan had just asked about how to deal with an issue that had happened on Noah's school bus.

"You can certainly talk to his teacher or school counselor," she said, "and ask them to emphasize that all families are unique and perfect as they are.

My mother asked teachers if she could come in and read books about adoption to the class."

"Did you like that?" Evan watched her curiously from his end of the couch. He sat facing her, one knee on the seat cushion, his left arm along the back of the sofa. Brown hair shot through with gold and red curled over the collar of a thin navy turtleneck that set off his robin's-egg-blue eyes. He wore dark-hued jeans that molded to his hips and thighs. Leaner than his very buff brother, who had a regimented weights-and-machines workout, Evan's fit body was more the result of running after Noah and an array of sports he truly enjoyed.

Curled into her side of the couch, Nikki relaxed in the ultrasoft sweats she'd been wearing when Evan texted. Her hair—black as ink, but streaked with russet highlights she was growing out—sat twisted into a haphazard topknot, and she hadn't worn a lick of makeup all day. She could feel the tingling relief of being able to talk and visit with Evan easily again. They hadn't fully addressed the fact that her family now thought of them as a couple, or that, for the first time two years, he'd brought up their single night of sex. There were definitely a couple of elephants in the room. Talking about something they both could agree on—Noah's need for support—seemed like the safest topic.

Responding honestly to Evan's last question, she said, "Only in the very early years. After second grade or so, I wanted to be like all the other kids. Having my mom come into the class and point out that I'm adopted made me want to crawl into a hole, frankly, which was the opposite of what she intended, of course."

"Yeah, of course." Evan rubbed the back of his neck. "Damned if you do, damned if you don't. Parents are screwed."

"Pretty much."

"So what do I do?"

He was truly asking, genuinely frustrated and wanting to try his very best for Noah. She loved that about her friend. No one who knew him would doubt for an instant that he'd skydive without a parachute for that kid.

"Listen to him," Nikki advised. "Validate his emotions, which are real, even if you don't agree with his thinking or his conclusions. Usually, it's not the circumstances in our lives that bother us—it's the way we think about those circumstances. But you are not going to persuade a six-year-old of that, or, quite frankly, a ten-, twelve- or sixteen-year-old, so don't try. Just be there. And model your own resilience when you can."

"Pretty useful, that psych degree of yours."

"Yeah. Too bad it's so hard to apply to myself."

The smile he gave her was fond and warm. It reached his eyes. "I guess that's par for the course in life."

"Yup."

These were the moments Nikki didn't want to give up. They used to sit on this couch after Noah went to bed and have a deep talk, sit in companionable silence or share the uncertainties that came with single parenting (for him) and dating (for her).

Evan Northrup might look like a cross between an action hero and a *GQ* cover model, but underneath all that hotness, he was as human as she and unafraid to show it. With her, at any rate—when he was at school or out and about in the community, he came across as confident, carefree, almost glib.

"How's the brandy?" she asked, noticing he hadn't had more than a sip.

Throwing a surprised frown at the snifter into which he'd poured a couple fingers' worth of liquor, Evan leaned forward to pick up the glass, warming it in his palm before he swirled and took a sip, his gaze on her. "It's excellent. Very smooth." Maintaining eye contact, he held the snifter out to her. "Do you want to try it?"

Déjà vu. It hit Nikki like a ton of bricks.

Two years ago, she'd been at home at eight o'clock on a Saturday night, quietly minding her own business and catching up on *Married At First Sight* when the phone rang.

"Want to come over to watch *Phantom of the Opera* and drink Negronis?" Evan's invite had caught her off guard.

"You're drinking Negronis?" she had asked him.

"No, *you're* drinking Negronis. I'm drinking Rémy Martin XO, neat."

He'd paused. "Or maybe a few tequila shots." Another pause. "Noah is on his first sleepover. Doing great, apparently. I, on the other hand, am… What's the hip way of saying I'm a fricking basket case? I don't like this feeling, Nikki. Can you come over and distract me?"

They'd met only a few months earlier at the Education and Equity conference in Portland. Right away, Nikki had liked his brain, the way he thought about social matters, his dedication to teaching. She'd wanted to size him up based on his extraordinary good looks and confidence, but he wouldn't fit neatly into the categories in her brain. For example, he wasn't great looking, confident and cocky; he was great looking, confident, curious and humble.

Evan had been the one to suggest they get together for coffee; that's when she'd discovered he was a devoted father as well.

Had she been attracted to him physically? Yeah. Romantically? No. He had an ex-wife he seemed too pained to discuss even though he hadn't seen her since shortly after their son's birth.

She'd gone to Evan's house that night two years ago, because she'd known how madly in love he was with his son, how important fatherhood was to him and she'd been able to imagine how challenging it was to parent alone.

She'd gone because he'd needed her.

Also, by that time, she'd loved him as a friend. They talked school life, brainstormed problems with students, agreed that Noah's preschool photo was the cutest in the class and that it wasn't really worth waking up on Saturday morning unless bagels and cream cheese were involved. They'd vibed. So, she'd gone over to his place to distract him.

They'd eaten Chicago corn, imbibed some alcohol—though not enough to claim inebriation—and watched *When Harry Met Sally*, because it had been on TV and she loved it. They'd commented the whole way through. When Harry and Sally slept together, they had sung the "Say No" song from *Hamilton* and laughed until their stomachs hurt.

Then Evan had offered her the brandy snifter he'd been holding and asked, "Want a taste?"

That was the *déjà vu* part. What had happened next would not happen again today.

She'd taken the snifter, holding his gaze the way he was holding hers right now as she'd taken a sip. The brandy had warmed the back of her throat and created a delightful trail of heat down to her belly.

After that, it was kind of hard to figure out who had done what.

To this day, Nikki thought he'd moved toward her

first…but maybe they'd moved toward each other? In any case, they'd kissed—on the lips, instead of the cheek as they had done occasionally when greeting each other.

Having just watched *When Harry Met Sally*, they ought to have learned a little something. Once a relationship crossed the line, it crossed the line for good.

When she'd dissected the event afterward—and she had, several times—there had been a moment… although perhaps it had been too short to refer to as a "moment," but a flicker, nonetheless…of time during which the thought *we shouldn't be doing this* had flooded her brain. Unfortunately, her libido had shoved the thought out of the way.

They hadn't talked about how stupid they were being. Instead, the kiss had kept going on and on until Evan had lifted his head at one point and asked, "Yes?"

She did not say, "NO!" like in the *Hamilton* song.

Instead, she'd breathed out, "Yes," because her lady parts had felt more alive and happy than they'd ever felt and threatened to turn in their resignation immediately if she denied them this one small thing.

Evan had stood up from the couch and swooped her up in his arms. Really. Just like in the movies. She'd weighed one hundred and forty-seven pounds that morning (she tended to remember life's biggest moments by what she'd weighed that day) and the

Chicago corn could not have helped. Still, he hadn't hesitated one bit.

At five feet one half inch tall, she'd been at her heaviest after her most recent breakup and felt self-conscious as hell.

On the way to Evan's bedroom, the lady parts had spoken up again, warning, "Do not think about anything except how good this feels, or we swear we're through with you."

A little harsh, but she'd heeded the challenge. She'd been thirty-five at the time, hadn't dated anyone in over a year, and despite multiple attempts to diet and exercise her way to sexual confidence, the only parts of her body that appeared to be shrinking were her ovaries. If that wasn't cause for concern, she didn't know what was. Couple that with a little alcohol and the influence of Harry and Sally, and you had a recipe for...

Very.

Good.

Sex. With a friend.

It wouldn't be too off base to claim, *remarkably good sex with a friend*. That had been her take on it, at any rate.

The next morning the fear had come crashing down. Evan didn't like to talk about his former marriage except to say that marriage was one of life's greatest gifts and that Mikaela had left him, not the other way around. All these years later he still didn't date and had no interest in marrying again. Nikki and Evan had certainly not been dating; they had just fallen into sex.

Nikki, however, wanted to be with a partner long-term (some length of time between the-rest-of-her-life and eternity seemed about right).

Mix together all those ingredients and you had a recipe for heartbreak. So, the morning after the night before, it had made absolute sense to be the first one to be crystal clear that the naked part of their relationship was O-VAH. He'd have done it eventually if she hadn't.

Staring at the brandy snifter Evan held out to her now, Nikki tried to picture skull and crossbones. "No thank you." Time to wrangle the elephant in the room. "Thank you for stepping in with my family. I do appreciate it. But it can't work."

Seated on the burgundy leather couch, with a large-framed window behind him, Evan looked mildly bemused. "Why not?"

"For one thing, it takes us both out of the dating pool. And I want to be in the dating pool."

"So soon?"

"Yes." She'd given it some thought. "Not tomorrow, but…soon. I want to be married. I want to have a family. I am not afraid to say that." Slapping the back of her right hand against her left palm as she repeated her goals, she said, "I want marriage. I want a family. Sadly, I may have to date someone first."

"'Sadly'? I thought you liked the idea of dating. You're always trying to set me up."

"That's because I was with somebody. I thought I was happy. I wanted everybody else to be happy. Now I'm stuck back in the stupid dating world, and I am sick and tired of dating. I don't want to go to bars. I hate scoping out guys at the gym or being scoped out. I don't want to go on *The Bachelor* and get engaged to someone who slept with five other people then put on his tie and asked me to marry him, and I don't believe *Love Is Blind.* So unless I'm willing to let my parents arrange a marriage for me, I'm stuck. I have to get out there again and date."

"And my being your temporary fake boyfriend would spoil all the fun you're about to have?"

Nikki felt her body slump against his sofa cushions. "I'm about to turn thirty-seven. My uterus contracts just thinking about it. I can't kid myself that I have all the time in the world. I don't. Plus, I live in a town where the dating pool wouldn't fill a goldfish bowl. I'm in trouble."

Setting his snifter on the coffee table, Evan took one of her hands in both of his. "You're in a lot less trouble than you think. Men check you out all the time. You don't have an expiration date, Nikki. You're fine wine."

A small sincere smile hovered around his lips, and his gaze was steady and caring and sexy as hell. *Ach!* Why did he have to be so…perfect? Leaning closer to her now, he smelled like fresh laundry. She wasn't sure whether he wore some terrific light cologne or took multiple showers a day, but it seemed Evan always smelled clean. Clean and warm.

"To be honest," he mused, rubbing the back of her hand with his thumb, "I think your concerns speak to the wisdom of pretending to date me. It's a fact that employers discriminate against jobless candidates. Human bias. Walk into a wedding—or, frankly, anywhere—with a boyfriend in the background and you've upped your ante."

Her expression must have conveyed her distaste for that theory, because he let go of her and raised his hands. "Don't shoot the messenger." Picking up the snifter again, he drained it then gave her the characteristic easygoing smile that usually relaxed her.

Decidedly not relaxed this time, she asked, "Why do you want to do this? I mean, assuming I see your point about it being to my advantage—and I'm not saying I do—what's in it for you?"

Stretching his arms then crossing them behind his head, Evan appeared to consider his response. "Did you ever feel responsible for your younger siblings when they messed up in school, especially with a teacher you really liked?"

"Yes."

"It's like that. I really like you, Drew screwed up, he's my dumbass younger sibling, I feel responsible. Even though I'm not," he added before she could refute that. "Mostly it's because you're my friend. I knew you first." His voice lowered. "I don't want you to struggle through Gia's wedding, Nik. Let me help."

She wasn't entirely certain what she'd wanted him to say, but she didn't think that was it, because she felt...dull and kind of depressed.

"So, my brother," he interrupted her thoughts. "Did he really break off your engagement because you eat carbs?"

She knew Evan would take her side in the breakup. He might profess a sense of responsibility for Drew, but for as long as she'd known the Northrup brothers, there had also been a keen sense of competition between them. Drew was driven—by personal goals, by money, by a desire to be seen and known and respected by a multitude. Social media was made for personalities like his.

Evan, on the other hand, was driven by a need to teach, to share ideas and to be a responsible, values-forward person. Their father, Steven, leaned heavily in the direction of his younger son. A business mogul himself, with several franchised beauty-sculpting salons, he took great interest in Drew's extravagant growth plans for LeanUp With NorthrUp. On the other hand, Jason diminished Evan's work anytime it came up. To him, a teacher's salary amounted to wasted earning potential.

Oh, the family dinners Nikki had loathed, because of Steven's disrespect toward his older son. Drew and Evan's stepmother had been no help at all. Formerly a "tanning specialist," she was far more intrigued by Drew's efforts to beautify bodies than by Evan's efforts to teach a bunch of eighth graders the difference between a dependent and independent clause.

Evan mostly took it in stride, smiling his way through dinners, tossing attention Noah's way. Clearly present because he believed his son needed grandparents, not because he derived much pleasure from his family, Evan generally seemed to take the Northrups for who they were, balancing acceptance and detachment a lot better than she had. Coming from the boisterous, emotional, loving—and, sure, hovering—Chois, Nikki seemed to be more bothered by Evan's lack of a supportive family than he was. Everyone deserved to be seen, to be heard and appreciated. It drove Nikki batty to watch Evan's family underappreciate him.

She didn't want to add to his problems with the Northrups by making him take sides in her relationship with her ex-fiancé.

"Drew made a good point," she said. "If I was

hiding something as fundamental as what I eat, there's a disconnect between us."

"No question. You could have talked about it. Found out why there's a disconnect. Get marriage counseling if you needed to."

"Is that what you did?" She'd never asked before. Instantly, Evan's expression closed off.

"No," he admitted after a time. "Both people have to agree. I imagine that would have been an issue between you and Drew as well. He didn't give the two of you a chance."

"Have you talked to him about it?"

"I don't have to. I know my brother." The classic lines and angles of Evan's face looked harder than usual.

"It doesn't matter. It's better this way." She didn't believe that yet, but she would eventually.

Evan, on the other hand, was more unequivocal. "I don't doubt it. The question is why were you with him in the first place?"

"Sheez. What am I supposed to say to that? I fell in love with him. Obviously."

"Bull."

"I beg your pardon?" Evan liked jazz, which was playing in the background, but not loudly enough for her to have heard him incorrectly. "You're questioning *my* feelings for *my* fiancé."

"Yeah."

Nikki looked at him incredulously. "That's it—

'yeah'? As if you think you know me better than I know myself. You realize how arrogant that sounds, right?"

"I imagine it does. And before you point out—correctly—that I'm a fine one to talk, I agree with you. There isn't a single Northrup male who has a decent track record with women, and unfortunately I'm no exception. Which brings me back to my question: What were you doing with Drew? You have an MA in school counseling. He has the emotional IQ of a pencil."

Nikki's jaw dropped. "That's a terrible thing to say."

"Terrible or untrue?"

"It's an exaggeration." Drew had dumped her; even though it had just happened, she was already tired of people assuming their relationship had been a mistake from start to finish. "I was happy with Drew at first. Yes, he's more focused on the physical than the emotional, but he *is* capable of love, Evan. He wanted a relationship, and, yes, it was a struggle for him at times to be fully available, but I had my faults, too. At least he wanted to try." *Which is more than you want to do with...anyone.*

She wasn't going to say that. It had no bearing on anything. Evan, however, got her point: He'd stepped over the line.

"Daddy!"

Noah's voice called out in sleepy need.

Evan looked from her toward the direction of Noah's bedroom, then back to Nikki.

"Daaaad!"

"I don't want him to get out of bed."

She nodded. "Go."

Running fingers through the thick curls that barely moved, Evan looked at Nikki somberly. "Can you stay?"

"No. School night. I should get home. I'm sorry I said—"

Obviously wanting to say something more, but refraining, he shook his head. "No worries. School night for me, too."

"Dad?"

Evan rose.

Nikki followed. She'd come over here hoping to mend a fence. Instead, it felt as if they'd erected a brick wall between them.

Was this how it was going to be from now on? She and Drew broken up, and she and Evan never the same again?

She'd started the year with the sense of belonging she'd always craved. After she married Drew, she'd have a husband and a potential family of her own. She was going to be Eden's *engaged* maid of honor and then Eden was going to be the matron of honor at *her* wedding.

That had been the plan.

Now? She felt as if she was at square one again,

staring thirty-seven in the face with no husband, no future babies of her own, no nephew named Noah.

And no best friend brother-in-law she could count on being in her life forever.

Chapter Six

Leo's Tavern was full and noisy on the Thursday after Nikki left Evan's house. The two of them hadn't spoken since, and the ensuing days had been…well, crappy, frankly. Nikki had been tearful, grumpy and anxious.

She'd have to live in denial not to be aware that her dreams of love and a family of her own we're inching away, not moving closer as she approached forty. Only three more years until her chances dropped by several percentiles.

"Should we get a platter of Irish nachos for the table?" Minniver Casey, principal at the high school that served Holliday, Wurst and a couple of smaller townships, asked the six women who occupied two tables pushed together in the center of Leo's moodily lit bar and eatery. The assembled group had no connection to the high school, save for Minn and Nikki. Tonight's gathering was supposed to be a support group of sorts, although in Nikki's mind, support groups were intended to make people feel better, not worse. A discreet glance at her watch told Nikki she'd been here forty-five minutes and so far, the only thing she'd gotten out of it were several reasons to restart therapy.

When a waitress passed by, Minn ordered Leo's famous Irish nachos—skinny fries, two kinds of cheese, scallions and homemade ranch dressing to dip them in. At the far end of the table, a woman with long dark hair and purple lipstick requested tequila shots for everyone. Only Nikki and Minn declined, having previously concurred that the local high school principal and guidance counselor knocking back tequila shots on a school night would not be a great look. Especially as they'd both recently been dumped by their respective partners.

"A toast," Minn said, raising a glass of ginger ale while the others hoisted margaritas that were nearly drained. "Thank you for inviting me to join this group when I was at my absolute lowest, and thank *you*," she angled toward Nikki, who sat beside her, "for joining us tonight. What brought us here sucks, but together we are stronger and smarter than we are on our own."

"Hear, hear," agreed the woman with purple lipstick, whose name was Anya.

A slender, sweet-looking blonde who had introduced herself as Patience added, "Love sucks. So does the idea that we need a partner to be happy. We don't have to buy into that provincial tripe anymore. Am I right or am I right?"

"You're right!" the women chorused.

Oh, gosh.

"To the Angosturas!" a woman sitting next to Anya cheered.

"The Angosturas!" replied the others, drinking then embarking on a discussion about the best place to buy postbreakup "trashy lingerie."

Nikki leaned toward her friend and boss. "Why do they call themselves the Angosturas?"

"It's code. Angostura bitters are liquefied herbs and spices you can find in lots of alcoholic drinks. Tames the sweetness. We meet in a bar, we're bitter and should probably get over it, but we're not ready. Not yet, anyway." She leaned closer to Nikki. "OTOH, who wants to be known as The Bitters. Right?"

"Well, yeah," Nikki agreed. According to Minn, all the members of the Angostura Bitters Club had been left by a spouse or partner. Some lived in Holliday, but not all. "You know," she said, stirring her virgin piña colada, "considering that I'm the guidance counselor at your high school, I'm not sure I should commit to bitterness as a way of life."

Grabbing a handful of Leo's house-roasted spicy peanuts, Minn started munching. "I hear you. I do rely on you for perspective and equanimity at work. As a fellow dumpee, however, I'd hate to rob you of the opportunity to really revile Drew with no one to tell you to tone it down."

Digesting her role as "fellow dumpee," Nikki nodded while her mood plummeted to the soles of her feet. "I appreciate that."

Forty-nine years old, brilliant at managing a school full of teens and stressed-out adults, Minn had been depressed, restless and irritable since her husband left her for his much younger mistress three months prior. She'd never been that way before. Her presence was considered a comfort to staff and students alike. Sure, she was tough when she needed to be, but empathy and compassion had been her guideposts. Scott's lies and betrayal had changed her. Heartache scratched away at a person, like scars on a wood table.

"I think the worst part of being left is the self-doubt," Nikki said to Minn, rather than to the table at large.

After another handful of peanuts, Minn reached for her ginger ale and stared at the tiny bubbles. "Yeah."

"Have any of the Angosturas figured out how to counter that?"

"Mmm-hmm." She took a sip of the ginger ale, swallowed and said, "Sex. Apparently."

"Oh. Alrighty. I was expecting, you know, therapy or a new hobby. But sex…" Nikki nodded, reaching for her drink and thinking maybe she should have opted for alcohol, school night or not. "So, not an actual relationship?"

"No. Too many emotions involved. Too threatening. Just sex with someone who can't hurt your heart."

"Gotcha. I've never been one for casual sex," Nikki said. Except of course for her one departure with Evan. "Have you…gone that route?"

Before she could answer, Leo, the bar owner himself, arrived at their table. Standing beside Minn's chair with two heaping platters of food, he said, "I believe you ordered these."

Nikki couldn't help noticing that Minn instantly hunched her shoulders and lowered her head, keeping her gaze strictly away from Leo. Which was weird, because, before her faithless husband's departure, they had a standing Friday-night date at the tavern.

"We sure did," replied Anya. "And tequila shots." She tilted her head, openly assessing the man who had once played halfback for the Seattle Seahawks. "But now that I think of it, Jell-O shots would be much more interesting. Especially if you have two free tables we can push together and you're willing to lie down on them."

Minn choked so hard on her ginger ale that some spurted out her nose.

Nikki didn't know Leo well. The tavern was a popular meeting spot, and she'd come in here plenty of times, but Leo was not your typical tell-me-all-your-troubles-and-have-another-round kind of bartender. His frame was broad enough to balance a tray of nachos on each of his massive shoulders, and she imagined the rest of his body was pretty fit, too, beneath the loose Pendleton shirts he favored. He had a full head of sandy-brown waves, though the hairline was beginning to recede a bit. Nikki guessed him to be in his forties. If he dated, either women or men, she hadn't heard anything about it. He'd owned the tavern for at least a decade and a half, which was a few years before she'd moved here. He must have received some propositions in that time. At present, he didn't appear interested at all in Anya.

"I don't stock Jell-O." He looked down. "Minn, you need anything else?"

Minn looked up at him, seeming startled. "No. Nope. Which rhymes with pope." She released a trill of uncomfortable laughter. "I'm good. Great!" Swiftly, she looked down again.

In this lighting, Nikki couldn't be sure, but she

thought Minn was blushing. And no wonder. *Nope.*
Which rhymes with pope?

"I'll have Jessenia bring your shots," Leo said.
The man had a gift for speaking without a smile on
his face or in his voice. He sauntered back to the bar.

Minn sank into the chair, looking as if she
wished the floor would open to swallow her and
the remains of her dignity.

"Ooh, here comes good trouble." Patience was
staring toward the door, through which a tall dark-
haired man had just entered. "I'd do Jell-O shots off
his abs anytime." She made a slurpy, sucking sound.
Gross.

The "dude" in question happened to be Gideon
Bowen, Eden's fiancé. The only man in town who
appeared more somber than Leo, Gideon possessed
a Severus Snape exterior over a heart full to burst-
ing with love for Nikki's BFF. Eden had waited a
long time for a love like the one she'd found with
Gideon. Planning their wedding filled her with a
joy Nikki had never witnessed in her before. She
frowned at Patience. *Hands off, lady.*

Catching Gideon's eye, Nikki waved. He responded with a genuine smile, but his quick glance
around the table told her he wasn't planning to come
over. Town doctor or not, Gideon wasn't an extro-
vert, though under Eden's influence he'd warmed
up his persona.

Settling for the smile, Nikki watched him walk

to the bar and trade a few words with Leo, who then walked toward the kitchen. It wasn't hard to deduce why Gideon was here. Eden adored Leo's burgers and fries. Although Gideon was Holliday's self-appointed nutritionist, and rarely touched sugar or red meat himself, he wisely chose to overlook his beloved's lust for junk food from time to time and was likely bringing a sautéed-mushroom-onion-avocado burger home for her. Extra special sauce for the fries. Now that was love.

A mélange of gratitude for her friend's good fortune in finding her *bashert*, her soul mate, yearning to find her own and a healthy dollop of envy made Nikki's chest feel tight. Eden and Gideon had seemed like opposites in every way, yet here they were, solid in a relationship everyone believed was going to last. They'd both known pain in their lives. After years of shouldering it on their own, sharing it had given birth to a true pairing of soul mates.

Nikki hadn't had that with Drew. On some level, she must have known it all along. Her relationship with Drew had been exciting, even thrilling at times. She'd liked who she was when she was with him—physically strong, more carefree, sexy. She'd liked the feeling of being on top of the world, with nothing more to want.

"Hoo, mama, there's another one!" This time a woman named Felice straightened in her chair, looking a lot less bitter than she had earlier as she ogled the newest arrival to Leo's Tavern.

Oh, cripes. Evan.

Tomorrow was an in-service day at the elementary school—no classes—and Noah was on a sleepover tonight with one of his buddies from Pee Wee league. Nikki had forgotten. Wouldn't have expected Evan to come to Leo's alone, though. Usually, when Noah wasn't home for one reason or another, Evan asked Nikki to hang out.

Watching his progress through the crowded tavern, she saw him pause at a table to talk to a group of guys who played softball with him every Saturday. Looked as if he might be there to meet them. Typically, Evan joined their games a couple times a month while Nikki hung out with Noah at the adjacent park so they could practice their Rollerblading skills.

Pressing on to the bar, Evan clapped Gideon on the shoulder. She had introduced Evan to Eden, and they'd bonded over a shared love of local authors and history. Later, Evan had asked Gideon to speak to his eighth graders about medical careers, and poof!—a brotherhood was formed.

When Leo came over to take Evan's order, the show of friendship continued with a thumb-linking handclasp. Somehow, Nikki hadn't realized Evan and Leo were pals, though it made sense as Leo, too, played softball from time to time.

"Mmm-mmm-mmm," Anya growled like a lioness. "That is the yummiest group of single men I've seen in a long time. Per suggestion number three on the Angostura list of bitter-calming activities, I propose that three of us lock down some sexy time with those fine, fine specimens."

"Is this a support group or desperate horny singles club?" Nikki asked Minn, her irritation mounting. No way was anyone from this table going after Gideon.

Withholding none of her outrage, she said loudly and clearly, "They are not all single. The gentleman with the black hair?" She pointed toward the bar. "He is not single."

Anya smiled quickly, then blinked her heavily lashed eyes slowly. "Calm down, sweetie. He's single tonight."

"He's *engaged* to a friend of mine." Shoving back her chair, Nikki rose to her full five foot half inch. "Tonight and every night. *Sweetie.*"

Beside her, Nikki felt Minn perk up. At school, Nikki was the poster child for proper use of de-escalation techniques.

Anya's jaw fell open in mocking disbelief. "Seriously? Your friend needs you to puppy guard her boyfriend? I think you've joined the wrong playgroup. We're all grown-ups. When we see something—or someone—we want, we feel entitled to go after it.

Just like our exes did." Shoving back her own chair, she stood to confront Nikki from across the table.

"You go after what you want no matter whom it hurts? Really? You just behave however you want and screw everyone else, like the people who dumped on us?" Nikki looked at Minn. "What the hell, Minn. You actually like these people?"

Anya's smokey eyes glittered. She pointed a finger at her own chest. "I spent my entire life pleasing everyone but myself. It got me nowhere, except in line for SNAP benefits so I could feed three kids on a receptionist's salary while the perfect husband and father moved to the Bahamas with the wife of the youth pastor at our church!" As Anya's voice rose, Nikki could feel the eyes of the people at the surrounding tables. "You don't want me to go after your friend's man? Fine. Whatever." She tossed an artificially dark ponytail over her shoulder. "He's not the only man here, and my kids are at their grandparents all weekend. This girl's going to have some fun. For a change."

After Anya's speech, Nikki felt for her, but she sure as heck didn't trust the woman. "If that's how you want to spend your night, great. Leave here with anyone you want who wants to leave with you." She pointed to the men at the bar. "But it won't be one of them."

Anya laughed. "Wanna bet?" She started walking.

The panic that coursed through Nikki in that

moment felt hot and engulfing. Moving faster than Anya, darting around tables and chairs, Nikki bee-lined it to the bar.

"Hi, boys," she said the second she got there. "Busy night in here, huh, Leo?" She could sense Anya hot on her heels. "Gideon, you're picking up something for your *fiancée*, I bet. A Leo Special burger, am I right? I love the way you two know each other so well and are always trying to please one another."

Evan arched his brow, clearly insinuating her de-meanor was...weird. She ignored him. It wasn't that she thought Gideon would cheat on Eden, or even be tempted. But the thought that someone might think it was okay drove her nuts. "A true love like yours is rare. It ought to be valued and protected," she asserted firmly, "not only by the two of you, but by everyone around you. We should all help you value and protect it."

Gideon looked bemused. He wasn't one to in-volve himself in local drama. "Thank you. That's very thoughtful."

"Of course," she said as Anya sidled up, posi-tioning herself between Nikki and Evan. Now that they were both standing, damn she was tall. Nikki glanced down. Mile High stilettos launched her to at least five foot ten inches, maybe six feet. She was ultra-thin, too, her sheath dress wrapped around her like a glove. She hooked one thin arm through Evan's. He looked more amused than unhappy.

"Hey, fellas," she said to the group then turned her face toward Evan's. "What brings you here tonight, Ev?"

Ev? "You two know each other?"

Anya looked down, way way down, at Nikki. "I work for his accountant." She returned her attention to Evan. "You're our favorite client."

Evan treated her to an amused smile. "Is that so. Well, I believe that's the nicest thing I've heard all week."

Anya responded by practically humping the biceps of her office's favorite client.

"Looks like your order's up," Leo told Gideon. "I'll be right back."

Gideon turned toward Nik. "Eden tells me you and she are having a last-hurrah sleepover next weekend to mark the end of your single days. Is it going to get wild?"

Nikki squelched a wince. She'd forgotten about that. Eden must not have told her husband-to-be about the end of Nikki's engagement. Did she want to explain the situation here, with Evan and his barnacle standing by? No, she did not.

"It could get pretty wild. You never know."

"Speaking of festivities," Anya cooed, her bosom stuck like a suction cup to Evan's upper arm, "as fun as it is here, I bet we could have a lot more fun at my place." Nikki doubted that Anya could see clearly through her false eyelashes, but the look she gave Evan could set a man on fire. Just because Evan didn't *date* much did not mean he didn't have sex.

"Thanks for the invitation," he said. "But I'm here to meet some friends." Nikki felt tremendous relief. Anya was the worst possible choice for him. He nodded to the table of fellow softball players. "Want to join us?"

No. Might as well ask a puppy if it wanted to play tug-o'-war.

Anya appeared only slightly disappointed that he hadn't jumped at her offer. Resilient, she turned her attention to sitting with an entire tableful of men. "OK," she agreed. "As long as I can sit near you."

Evan said nothing, but smiled.

Returning with Gideon's order, Leo told Nikki, "Your tequila shots are still on the bar waiting to be served." He jerked his head to where a tray with four shots waited. "Sorry about that. We're short-handed. I'll bring them over."

Picking up his bag of food, Gideon said his good-byes and headed out, a man who knew where he was going and was happy about how he was going to spend his night.

That left Evan, Anya and Nikki, who loathed the idea of Anya glued to her friend. It wasn't that she didn't want Evan to be with someone…but someone sensible and cautious, who would be in it for the right reasons and take things slowly, if only for Noah's sake.

Would Evan truly consider a one-night stand or a fling with the leader of the Angostura Bitters?

"Can I steal you for a minute?" she asked Evan.

"Sure."

Anya gave Nikki a salty glare, but all she said was "I'll be waiting," with a promise in her voice.

Detaching himself from Anya's décolletage, Evan followed Nikki to the area of the tavern where a pool table and other games offered a diversion. Once they were standing in a relatively quiet spot, Nikki realized she had no idea what to say.

Evan filled the silence. "You found a new social group. Good for you."

His eyes glinted with the humor she'd always found so damn appealing. She nodded. "Yeah. I'm especially looking forward to celebrating the holidays with them."

"I'm sorry about the other night." He tucked his head and raised his brow, an expression she often saw in Noah as well. "You were hurting over Drew, and I was arrogant."

Hurting over Drew? Yes, she had to be hurting over Drew, didn't she?

Standing here, though, in Leo's, with the sounds of laughter and conversation, the click-clack-click of billiard balls smacking each other on the way to a pocket, and Leo's voice raised to call out an order of nachos for the bar, she didn't want to be hurt. Or pathetic. Or bitter. She wanted to be fun and hip and *chosen*—the way she'd felt as Drew's fiancée.

Being the jilted bride was no picnic. Like taking a hot poker and jamming it into her ego.

Vulnerability was supposed to be a positive thing, but sometimes it was excruciating.

"I think," she said carefully, aware that she wasn't nearly as in touch with her inner warrior as she wanted to be, "that what bothered me about our talk the other night was you intimated that you knew all along my relationship with Drew was going to fail. I never realized you felt that way. I thought…" Oh, crumb. Her eyes were beginning to sting. "Never mind. He and I weren't on the same page."

"Not on the same page about a food plan? Or not on the same page about life?"

"The latter. But apparently you knew that."

Evan's expression grew more serious. "You were too good for him." And then he smiled. "Too good for any Northrup."

Oh, wow. For a second it felt as if her heart was being vacuumed from her chest. "Not for Noah," she countered.

He chuckled. "True."

"Why do you put yourself in Drew's category?"

In a gesture that probably looked a lot more casual than it felt, Evan tucked Nikki's hair behind her ear. "Merely stating a fact. You're capable of forever.

Northrups tend to focus on 'for now' as the only manageable unit of time in romantic relationships."

"That's what you did?"

"It's what I do now."

Anya's laughter caught Nikki's attention before she could respond. The imposing woman had returned to their table and was currently downing a shot with the other Angosturas, her lash-fringed eyes trained on Evan, waiting to stake her claim. Anya's struggles had led her, too, to focus on *now*. All of Nikki's experience, on the other hand, pushed her to think about the future.

"I didn't thank you for offering to be my plus-one at Gia's wedding," she told Evan. "I'm sorry about that. I do appreciate it."

"You're welcome."

"And, you may be right."

Evan did not attempt to hide his surprise. "Really."

"Yes." She hadn't actually worked it out yet, but something about tonight…everything about tonight…was persuading her not to look a gift horse in the mouth. "I'd like to go to Gia's wedding with you. Actually, Eden's brother, Ryan, is getting married first, so…"

The half-smile on Evan's lips and the light in his eyes told her that after dissing his offer the first time, she was going to have to work for it a little. "So…?" he asked. "Are you inviting me? As your date?"

"My *fake* date, yeah." She smiled at his raised brow. "Evan Northrup, would you do me the very great favor and pleasure of being my pretend plus-one at Ryan Berman's wedding? It's in May."

"Let me check my calendar." She swatted his arm, gave him the exact date, and he laughed. "I'm sure that'll work out."

"Great. Thank you."

"Of course."

She glanced at the table where the Angosturas seemed to be getting a bit tipsy and much louder now, except for Minn, who nursed her ginger ale and looked miserable.

"Minn looks like she needs company," Nikki murmured.

Evan followed her gaze. "I'll walk you back."

When they arrived at the table, Minn looked up. "Hey, Evan. It's been a while."

He bent down to give her a quick hug. "How've you been, Minnie?"

"Peachy. How's life at the middle school? I keep thinking I should try to convince you to teach high school. I need a health teacher. You haven't lived until you've tried to explain how to unroll a condom to a group of hypersexual ninth graders."

"A persuasive argument."

Nikki sat down while Evan and Minn chatted briefly about the progress of a mentorship program Minn had initiated at the middle school shortly before she'd left to become principal of the high school. Nikki, meanwhile, kept her eye on Anya, who waited impatiently for him to finish with Minn. Despite multiple tequila shots, the dark-haired woman maintained a laser-like focus on her target.

Anya was going to try to sleep with Evan tonight, no question about it. Sudden, red-hot resistance flowed like lava through Nikki's veins. It had nothing to do with the fact that they were going to pretend to be dating. Anya wasn't right for him, and she definitely was not right for Noah. Period.

Nonetheless, when Minn and Evan said goodbye, Anya was by his side faster than a cheetah after a guinea fowl.

As they walked together to the table of softball players, Nikki couldn't come up with a single thing to say to stop them.

"That's an unlikely pair," Minn muttered.

"No kidding." Thinking of something, Nikki turned to her friend and principal. "Did you ever meet Evan's ex-wife? Noah was still a baby when Evan came to work for the middle school, right?"

"I met her not too long after I hired him, but she didn't stick around." Minn pumped her straw in the ice of her ginger ale. "We had a staff bowling night at the start of the year, and she came. Reluctantly, I think."

"What did she look like?"

Minn eyed Nikki curiously. "You've never talked to him about this? I thought you two were besties."

"We are, but Evan doesn't talk often about that part of his life." Shrugging, she tried to keep her tone casual. "I'm curious. Evan doesn't date much. Just wondering if Anya is his type."

"Lord, I hope not! Mikaela wasn't anything like Anya. She was very wholesome looking. Zero makeup. Straight blond hair and very serious. Super quiet. She didn't seem affected or anything, just very bored with bowling and, you know, with her life in general if I'm being honest. It was hard not to notice. She was pregnant, but I don't think any of us were all that surprised when he came back to school single the following fall. What did surprise me was that he had full custody of their baby. She seemed to be totally out of the picture at that point. She was a field biologist, wasn't she? Or worked with gorillas, or saved rain forests or something?"

"I think she works with an organization that brings clean water to rural areas in Central America." Drew had told Nikki that.

"Mmm. What I remember is that we all thought she sounded fascinating on paper, but in person we kinda…"

"What?" Nikki knew she was fishing for gossip and felt appropriately shamefaced, but not enough to stop.

Minn shook her head. "Never mind. I'm so bitter now. It's awful, really. I used to be nice."

"You're still nice."

Sucking on her ginger ale, she countered strongly, "No I'm not. Happy people piss me off. Not the kids at school. I don't mean that. I mean, happy couples. Dating people. Or happily married people with families. And dogs. And minivans. We never needed a minivan. I really wanted one. And a five-pound jar of peanut butter."

"I didn't know you were that much of a peanut butter fan."

"I'm not. I don't want to *eat* five pounds of peanut butter—I want to look at it when I open my pantry. I want to know I need it." Her brown eyes grew misty. "You can freeze PB&J sandwiches—did you know that? I read it on a mom blog. That way, you pop them into lunch boxes at night, and they're ready to go the next day."

"Handy."

"Very. Did you want kids with the body builder?"

"He's a fitness instructor," Nikki murmured, evading the question. "He doesn't do competitions."

Minn shrugged. "Scott and his mistress are pregnant. Or, I guess she's not his mistress anymore now that he and I are divorced. She's his girlfriend. Partner. Main squeeze. Baby mama." Grabbing several fries glued together with cheese, Minn crammed them into her mouth, then, resting her elbows on the table, put her head in her hands. "I feel so alone," she said quietly.

Nikki reached over to squeeze her boss's forearm. Something more than empathy filled Nikki's chest. Kinship. She felt a sorrowful kinship with a woman who fantasized about love and children the way she did.

Minn used a napkin to dab beneath her eyes. "Why haven't you had kids?"

"I've never been married."

Minn looked at Nikki almost pityingly. "Shouldn't wait for that. Trust me. I've been in perimenopause for years." Raising her head, she looked beseechingly at Nikki. "It sneaks up on you, Nikki. Age does. Before you know it, your face starts to change. One day you won't recognize your reflection when you walk past a store window, but you'll tell yourself it's the lighting or the glass. Then it'll happen when you look in a mirror. Then it happens when you look in your husband's eyes. You don't recognize yourself there, either. That's the worst."

Minn reached for her soda again. Nikki wanted something much more potent than a virgin piña colada.

Reaching for the purse she'd slung over the back of her chair, Minn rose. "I'm quitting the Angosturas," she said to the table at large. "I'm already bitter enough." To Nikki, she said, "You're ten years younger than I am right?"

"Thirty-seven next month." At the moment, that sounded ancient. Perimenopause could be right around the corner.

"Twelve years younger than I am, then. Good for you. Imagine all the changes you can make in twelve years. I'm gonna head home."

The Angosturas were obviously insulted, muttering to each other as they watched Minn weave around the tables and out Leo's door. When Minn was gone, she felt them turn their gazes toward her, but her attention was already on the booth where Evan and Anya sat laughing with the group of softball players.

Anya had one long slender arm slung around Evan's shoulders. Once again, her bosom was attached to his side like a sucker fish suction-cupped to the glass wall of an aquarium. Could cause injury if you tried to pry her off. And... *Oh, no. Come on now...* She was circling his inner ear with her index finger.

Evan looked relaxed, more focused on a story one of the other men was telling than on Anya's antics, but neither did he rebuff them.

That kind of if-you-want-it-come-and-get-it overture was not something Nikki had ever tried before a first date. She didn't have the confidence to have foreplay with a guy's ear in a bar. And not just any guy's ear; Anya was seducing Evan's ear, and Evan was...objectively really hot. Everyone wanted Evan.

"If you're jealous, why don't you go over there and get what you want?" One of the Angosturas—Jillian?—smirked at Nikki from down the table.

Caught off guard and frankly appalled, Nikki gestured to Evan. "I'm not jealous. I'm friends with him."

"Really?" The blonde, who appeared to be in her late thirties, like Nikki, asked, "Then why don't you want him to have fun?"

What was she going to say to that? Fun was going on a picnic, boating at Detroit Lake or snowboarding on Mount Hood. Fun was not ear sex with someone you'd just met in a public bar!

Was it?

More importantly, was Evan having fun? By the looks of it, he wasn't *not* having fun.

That's it. Grabbing her purse, Nikki stood fast enough to make herself dizzy. "Nice meeting you." She nodded to the other women, not one of whom looked like *they* were having fun anymore. At the end of this evening, it appeared the only victory would be Anya's if, in fact, Evan went home with her.

And, if he did…

Well.

Squaring her shoulders, Nikki marched toward the exit, but pivoted before she reached the door and strode straight back toward Evan. When she was halfway there, he appeared to sense her and looked up. Their gazes locked. As she walked, neither of them looked away. He might have been a little surprised when she reached him, but she didn't give either of them time to ask questions. Clutching her purse in one hand, she used the other to cup the back of his head as she leaned down to plant a kiss squarely on his handsome lips. She felt him stiffen, caught off guard. Despite his surprise, Evan had very good, very kissable lips. With that thought, she brought the contact to a swift conclusion.

"See you soon," she said breathlessly, although she wasn't sure she'd intended the breathless part.

This time, Nikki made it to the door without stopping and without looking at the Bitters, though she could feel their stares. If Evan went home with Anya tonight, then he wasn't the man she thought he was.

And that wasn't bitterness talking.

It was pure, unadulterated green-eyed possessiveness.

Chapter Seven

After a long week at school and a long week personally as well, the last thing Evan needed was dinner at his father and stepmother's house. He'd been thinking about Nikki non-stop since the night at Leo's. The brief, mostly chaste kiss she'd given him had packed more of a wallop than Anya's hand, which had been rubbing his thigh half the night. He hadn't spoken to Nikki since. She hadn't called, and he wanted some time to think, but every time he tried his thoughts felt jumbled.

Feeling the way he did—off balance, restless—he should not be navigating a night with his father, but they had a standing once-a-month meal, which was the only time Noah saw his grandparents. However ineffective they were, Evan told himself they were better than nothing.

"Did you bring my swim trunks, Dad? Can we go in the big pool? I can swim by myself. I'm super good. I'm a seal now. That's better than an otter and way, way, way, way, way, *way* better than goldfish."

"You are a good swimmer," Evan answered his son as he parked his Subaru on the broad, paver-lined driveway leading to Steven and Sherry Northrup's massive Lake Oswego estate. "It's a little early still to swim. Grandpa hasn't heated the pool yet."

Calling Steven Northrup "Grandpa" felt like calling Voldemort "Teddy Bear." Warm and cuddly, Steven was not. Invariably, he wore slacks and a dress shirt to dinner in his own home and expected others to do likewise. With a head of hair that was still as full as his son's, weekly manicures and skin preserved by monthly facials and a helluva lot of manscaping, Steven looked like a sexy older model. He behaved like the CEO he was. Nine parts business, one part begrudging family man.

Noah looked disappointed for a moment, then brightened. "Does Grandpa have a teakettle? We could boil the water like when I took a bath that time when the heat was out."

"I'm afraid not, bud. The pool is too large to heat with a teakettle, but I like the way you think. We can ask Grandpa when he's heating the pool and see if we can come over and use it. How's that plan?"

"Not too good, Dad."

Putting his car in Park and reaching in back for the dessert he'd bought at Sweet Holly's, Evan side-eyed his son. "Right. Postponing fun—never a good idea." To a six-year-old, that was not a good plan, and Noah's expression reflected his disappointment. "Let's see if Grandpa and Sherry got new fish for their tank." Which stretched across an entire wall in their cavernous family room.

Evan always referred to his father's fifth bride by her first name. First of all, at twenty-six she was too young to be "grandma," and second, there was no telling how long this union would last—

Wait, yes, there was. The average duration of his father's five marriages was four-point-six years. Steven's marriage to Evan's mother—marriage number one—ended with her premature death when Evan was three. Beth and Steven were married eight years, making their relationship Steven's longest. Not even his father's affluent lifestyle could persuade the second-through-third Mrs. Northrups to stay, given Steven's increasing neglect, which tended to peak around year three. Once he'd hit adulthood, Evan had been forced to field angry or frantic phone calls from the soon-to-be exes. Wife number four had been determined to stay, which, rather than warming Steven's heart, had appeared to irritate him to the point that he'd offered her nearly twice the amount specified by their prenup to get her to leave. Evan doubted Sherry would be around to watch Noah turn ten. It was pathetic.

Why Steven felt it necessary to repeat the experiment over and over was anyone's guess. Evan had asked him, receiving only an enigmatic smile and the response, "I like the concept of marriage." If that was, in fact, the case, one would think he'd have the decency not to bastardize it.

Evan's single foray into married life had proven he was no better at it than his father, and that was enough for him. Now he kept things light, casual.

"Show me your best I'm-disappointed-but-I'll-have-a-great-time-anyway attitude, and we'll hit some golf balls on the putting green," Evan promised his son. 'Cause, yeah, there was a putting green, too.

Growing up in the lap of all that luxury, without the lap of a loving parent to balance it, had tainted Evan's view of privilege. His mother's parents had lived on their Social Security, yet every time they'd picked him up for a visit, and he'd walked into the dated ranch-style house they'd filled with photos and the sort of mementos his stepmothers would have Goodwilled in a heartbeat, Evan had felt at home in a way he never did when he was actually at home. He'd often wished he could live with his grandparents, but they'd never offered, and he hadn't asked, too afraid of rejection to give voice to the longing. He'd liked to imagine, though, that his mom had been just like them.

If he was a decent parent at all, he figured it was because he'd inherited something from his mother's side of the family. Today he focused on raising Noah and building a life that was as different from the way he'd grown up as he could possibly get.

Evan took Noah's hand as they walked up the stone walkway to the Northrup McMansion, passing Drew's coal-black Chevy Suburban that had LeanUp With NorthrUp, along with his website address stenciled on the driver's and front passenger side doors. The license plate read LEAN UP.

For two years, Nikki had been present at most of these interminable formal dinners, and that had made them much more bearable. More than bearable, actually. On the occasion his father had suggested that Evan consider putting his teaching credentials "to better use" by "leveraging them to join Drew's coaching team so you can run a few of the satellite gyms," Nikki had snorted a 2009 Pape Clement Blanc through her nose then said, "Sorry, I thought you suggested he should give up teaching."

She would not be here tonight, of course. Drew had not been in touch with Evan since the breakup, but obviously he knew where things stood. Did their father know yet, or would Drew make the announcement over dinner?

"I get to ring the doorbell! Can I?" Noah crowed as they reached the door.

"Go for it."

Gleefully, Noah jabbed the button then waited for Paul McCartney and Wings to sing "Let 'Em In." The musical doorbell was Stepmommy Sherry's latest "home upgrade."

Eustacia, the cook-housekeeper (another upgrade), invited them into the foyer, where she took the cake box from Evan before directing them to the living room, where cocktails were being served.

Steven stood at the wet bar, mixing drinks; Sherry reclined in the corner of a silky settee whose fabric was almost exactly the color of her pale peach complexion. Drew and a young, very fit woman in a skintight electric-blue dress sat thigh-to-thigh on the sofa.

They were holding hands.

"Hey, Noah!" Drew welcomed, a doting uncle approximately once a month.

Evan felt Noah's small hand tighten around his. They had discussed the fact that Nikki and Drew no longer planned to get married, but that Nikki would stay in their lives, just like before. Evan hadn't expected Noah to have a problem with his uncle Drew today; however, he also hadn't expected another woman to be present and obviously taking Nikki's place. One look at his son's protruding lower lip and furrowed brow told Evan that Noah was struggling with this latest development. Evan related, because so was he. The difference between father and son was that Evan still felt bound to be polite, whereas Noah felt no such compunction.

"They're holding hands!" If looks could burn, Drew's and the blonde's clasped hands would go up in flames.

Steven and Sherry ignored the comment and welcomed Noah in their classic restrained fashion.

"Hello, young man. Would you like a Roy Rogers?" Steven half turned to greet his grandson.

Sherry, who at twenty-six appeared to be approximately the same age as Drew's new friend, offered a perfectly veneered smile. "Noah, you cute thing, have you gotten taller?"

"Kids get taller. Old people shrink." Noah repeated the anecdotal information Evan had shared with him. When the room at large laughed, Noah sidled closer to his father.

"That's very observant," said Drew's companion, "but it's only partially true. Men and women both can avoid or minimize height loss by laying down plenty of good bone starting when they're your age by maintaining an alkalizing diet and strong exercise program all through their lives. Isn't that good to know?"

Drew's expression said, *Isn't she something?*

Noah looked up at Evan. "I don't know what she said. Can my Roy Rogers have two cherries?"

"You bet. Dad, make Noah's a double."

If Steven had an opinion about the absence of Nikki and her immediate replacement by a woman who appeared to be Drew's long-lost fraternal twin, he wasn't showing it. "Two cherries for Noah. Sherry and I are drinking vodka martinis. Are you indulging tonight?" he asked his elder son.

Blood boiling after a glance at the sofa, where Drew was now stroking the woman's arm, Evan replied, "I think I'd better."

As alcohol contained carbs "that convert quickly to sugar," Drew and his friend stuck to water with an alkaline pH.

After settling Noah on the floor with a puzzle, Evan sat in a chair, told Sherry her spring flower arrangements were very nice, then focused on his half-brother and said pointedly, "So. What's new?"

Possibly Drew was a true narcissist. Possibly he was simply too selfish to realize how his family—Evan, at least—would react to his bringing a new woman on to the scene without first explaining why he'd called off his engagement mere weeks before the wedding.

Beaming with pride, Drew stared lovingly into the eyes of his new…girlfriend? In-house dietician? "This is Regina," he introduced. "Reg, my brother, Evan. He's a teacher, too."

"You're a teacher?" Evan asked.

She offered a half smile. "I prefer the word *educator*. It sounds more respectful of my proteges."

Oh, boy. "As opposed to the word *students*?"

"Correct."

Tearing his gaze away from the woman who, Evan estimated, would be almost as tall as Drew when she stood up, Drew said, "Regina is one of the best. Her Great Glutes and Bammin' Biceps class always has a waiting list. Sherry, if you're interested, let me know—I think I can get you in." He winked.

Sherry seemed to take that as an insult. "I do Peloton."

"You work for Drew, then?" Evan asked Regina.

Meeting Drew's gaze and reaching for his hand with a confidence and steadiness Evan couldn't help but both admire and hate under the circumstances, Regina answered, "We work together."

Drew was besotted. Was he really going to brush over the question of where Nikki was? Out with the old, in with the new and not a concern for anything above his own interests? Apparently he didn't give a damn that their father had done the same thing with both of their mothers?

Steven and Sherry behaved as if nothing was amiss. Giving in to boredom, Sherry began to leaf through a magazine from a small table on her right. Steven busied himself with the drinks, looking as if he had other matters on his mind, though not the matter of where his almost-daughter-in-law might be. Fact was, Steven had never responded to Nikki's warm overtures. Sometimes it had been like watching a golden retriever puppy attempting to engage an irritated Afghan hound.

In Steven's eyes, Nikki suffered from the same unfortunate blemish as Evan: She cared more about her life's purpose than a six-figure paycheck. The Northrups couldn't relate to that. Steven had started an import empire by the time he was thirty. Over the years he'd diversified and recently sold his kingdom for eight figures. Drew's venture warmed his stone-cold heart.

Was Steven completely unconcerned about Nikki? That thought made Evan feel like a bull in a chute.

Without even bothering to hide his suspicion that the relationship with Regina predated the breakup with Nikki, Evan asked, "How long have you two worked together?"

Instantly, he knew he didn't have to hear the answer to know the truth. Drew's expression flashed concern—not guilt, not shame or regret—merely the concern that Evan might call him out in front of everyone, which his swollen ego would not tolerate.

Evan had no intention of calling him out here. Not because he gave a rat's ass about hurting his brother's or his father's feelings, but because he didn't want his son to witness the scene.

He knew his brother; if a conversation about

Nikki didn't happen now, it never would. Drew would convince himself that the relationship was in the past and leave it there. Rising from his chair, Evan crouched before his son. "Nice work on that puzzle, boy-o. Remember to put your Roy Rogers on the table when you're not drinking it. Uncle Drew wants me to show him how to attach a rain chain to the roof gutter."

"Like we got!"

"Exactly. We'll be right back."

"Okay."

Drew, who didn't know squat about home maintenance, gave his brother a sour look, but evidently wasn't prepared to chance Evan pursuing the topic of Nikki in front of their father. Giving Regina an overly hearty smile, he said, "Back in a sec, babe."

Babe. Right.

At least two generations of Northrup males should consider celibacy an act of civil service. Evan hoped like hell he could teach Noah a different set of values.

No worries about Regina feeling awkward when they left. She dove right in to conversation. "Steven, Drew tells me you you're interested in lowering your BMI for health reasons…"

Evan led his brother outside to the patio area.

Privilege and affluence were in full display out here in the backyard—or, as Drew's mother had enjoyed referring to it, "on the estate." Cynthia had been responsible for the full, travertine stone, outdoor kitchen and dining areas. She'd been wife number two, a nice enough woman, who had lasted longer than her successors.

"How's your mother?" Evan asked as he led them away from the family room and French doors, through which they could be seen.

"She's fine," Drew answered curtly. "Where are we going?"

"To the pool, so we can talk in private. Is Cynthia planning to stay in Greece?"

"I don't know. Maybe."

The brevity of his reply reminded Evan that his own seven-year stint as Cynthia's stepson had ended when her marriage to his father had. Steven had moved on to Bettina, wife number three, who'd remodeled the master bath.

"Look, let's make this quick, all right?" Drew complained as they walked through an archway cut into a wall of laurel on the way to the pool area. "We weren't planning to stay for dinner. I have an interview with *AM Northwest* tomorrow morning. I may be their new fitness expert."

Ordinarily Evan would have offered his congratulations. He wasn't feeling that magnanimous today.

He stopped walking when they reached the pool, an epic fifteen hundred square feet with an infinity hot tub and waterfall that spilled over river rock—

the brainchild of Lynsee, wife number four, who adored HGTV.

Since Drew was in a hurry, Evan cut to the chase. "Does Regina know you were engaged as recently as last weekend?"

"She's part of the LeanUp brand. She understands how things are."

"How, exactly, are things?"

Putting his hands on his leaned-up hips, Drew looked irritated. "You're not going to understand." He shook his big handsome head. "You're friends with Nikki. You spend more time with her than I did. Which is fine, because I'm trying to build something big. But Nikki was lying to me, man. Through our whole relationship. So don't come after me."

"Lying about what? Carbohydrate grams?"

Drew raised his hands up like stop signs. "I told you, you don't get it. I asked her to be my partner. When you're talking about marriage, it's about a lot more than whether you're good in bed together. I'm surprised you don't know that." He actually looked pitying, the son of a bitch. "I'm not just building a brand, I'm creating a world of achievers with fitness goals, people who want the best for themselves. No excuses."

"Didn't Nike already do that?"

Drew's flash of concern was almost comical. "We're not going to say it the same way. That was just an example. Anyway, Regina understands what I'm doing with my life. She supports my mission-driven values and world-building goals."

"Awesome. Hopefully she's also a fan of mega-lomania. You've been cheating on Nikki." There was no point in pretending that was a question. "Now you're telling yourself the typical self-serving Northrup bullshit for screwing over someone you didn't deserve in the first place."

"I didn't deserve her? Thanks for your support, *bro*." The sun was starting to set, but the fury on Drew's face was clear. "I appreciate the advice of a single father who doesn't know where his kid's mother is. Why don't you get your nose out of my affairs and have one of your own? 'Cause it doesn't look you're your ex-wife's coming back."

The two men were a similar height. However, at this moment Evan's outrage made him feel as if he was towering over his brother. "Do not ever comment on Noah's mother. Not in front of him, not if he's within a twenty-mile radius of you, not *at all*."

"Why? Because you know you've screwed up every relationship you've ever been in and don't want your son to know? You judge everyone! Maybe it's time you quit the holier-than-thou BS bro. By the way, this whole protector-of-womanhood gig you've got going—you might want to see a thera-pist about it. My guess is it has something to do with your mother."

The ability to maintain one's temper was a requisite for working in a middle school. Evan liked to think he was good at letting arrows bounce off him and fall to the ground, powerless. Typically, his mood darkened in defense of other people, not himself.

This was different.

He walked toward Drew, fists itching to wipe the smug look off his face. His mother was the only woman who'd married Steven before his bank accounts hit nine digits. Being loved during his first three years by someone whose heart hadn't been encased in a steel vault was pretty much the only hope he had that he wasn't like Steven or Drew. Narcissistic. Selfish. And in Drew's case apparently devoid of integrity.

"This is from Nikki. And me."

His fingers were curled into punching mode; his right shoulder and elbow cocked back. Drew was two inches taller and had a helluva lot more muscle, but Evan was quicker—mentally and physically—and he had the element of surprise.

His fist was flying at Drew before the other man guessed it was coming. But Evan had enough awareness to know he'd hate himself if they returned bloody and bruised to the house, and he had to explain to his son that he'd started it.

At the last moment, his fist connected hard with Drew's shoulder, knocking him off-balance so that he stumbled backward. It took only another small shove with both hands to push him into the expensive pool his mother had ordered.

It might not have felt as good as hitting him would have, but the splash Drew's dense body made and the stunned expression on his arrogant face as he came up sputtering was satisfying. Damn satisfying, indeed.

"Can everyone sit down?"

Sophie Wurst picked up the nearest utensil— a butter knife she'd used to cut her hamburger in half—and smacked it on the table like a gavel.

"Don't hit my table," Anthony Jackson, owner-proprietor of Wurst Burgers, protested. "You'll scratch it."

Nikki shared a glance with Mary Anna Stackler who then shared one with her twin sister, Leonora. The Stackler twins were seventy-six; some of the multitude of scratches on Anthony's tabletops were as old as they were.

"We need to stop gabbing, people." Sophie stood at five foot three when she kept her back perfectly straight, wore baggy jeans that made her look like a kid and had a halo of natural golden-blond curls that on anyone else would have seemed angelic. Sophie, however, also possessed an obsessive drive for vengeance that made her appear anything but. "You've all been eating and talking for forty minutes. That's enough. We've got to get down to business."

Nikki shook her head in exasperation. She'd given Sophie the you'll-catch-more-flies-with-honey talk numerous times. So had others. It never helped.

"This is the second meeting of the Small-Town Olympics trials, Pacific Northwest Division, Team Wurst. Come to order!" She picked up the knife again and rapped the table. Anthony pulled it from her hand and set it aside.

Several days after kissing Evan at Leo's, Nikki had yet to speak to Evan, but he was supposed to be here tonight. She was on pins and needles, waiting for him and was grateful for the distraction of this meeting.

Glancing around the tables Sophie had pushed together into a U configuration and counted ten people, including Anthony and the Stacklers, at this gathering of would-be athletes. Holliday entered a team in all the PNW Small-Town Olympic Games and medaled every time. They generated tourist dollars by turning trainings into community events and hosting citywide celebrations for their victorious athletes.

Wurst, on the other hand, had never had a team in the games. Sophie had asked Jeremy Holliday to partner with Wurst, its next-door neighbor, so the glory could be spread around, but Jeremy wanted

Sophie on his team about as much as a lion wants to chill with a hyena. Hence, Sophie's insistence on putting together Team Wurst and whipping team Holliday's collective tush. (Which was laughably unlikely, but Sophie didn't want to acknowledge that.)

Neither Nikki nor Evan lived in Wurst, proper, but Sophie had found a provision in the bylaws allowing county and city workers to participate on a team representing the population they served. Nikki, feeling empathy for an underdog, signed herself up. She'd dragged Evan along for companionship.

Looking around now, Nikki wondered if she and Evan might be the only members of the team who participated in sports on a regular basis. Anthony, who was in his mid-sixties and had permanent tobacco stains on his fingers, got most of his exercise dealing cards to his poker buddies on Friday evenings and looked as if a lap around the high school track could take him down. Karl Hansen, who owned Bookkeeping By Karl, belonged to a gym in Salem but had never gone beyond the free introductory workout, and Melody Buell, who taught Comparative Epistemology at Linfield University, was hoping that Kundalini yoga might be suggested as one of the events. There were a couple of other people here whom Nikki didn't know. Not nearly enough to accomplish what Sophie hoped to accomplish.

"Excuse me." A thin gentleman in his forties raised his hand. "I hate to interrupt, but—"

"Identify yourself for the minutes," Sophie instructed.

"No one is taking minutes," Melody noted.

"Someone needs to take minutes."

No one spoke up.

Sophie put her hands on her hips as she stood at the end of the table. "People—"

"I'll do it," Karl acquiesced reluctantly. "Tony, gimme that napkin. You got a pen?"

"You can't take the minutes on a napkin," Sophie protested, her frustration visibly mounting. "We have several agenda items—"

"Item numero uno—change the name of our team. No one wants to be on the 'Wurst team.' You know what I'm saying?" A heavy-set woman with a thick blond updo and an artificial flower behind one ear spoke up to nods around the room.

"Identify yourself for the minutes," Sophie reminded, trying to rein in her impatience.

"Flora Greely. I own Flora's, The Best Little Flower Shop In Wurst. The *only* flower shop in Wurst." Her booming laugh and obvious irreverence were pretty darn infectious.

"If I may circle back to the comment I was going to make," ventured the thin fellow Sophie had interrupted regarding the minutes. "For the minutes, my name is Charles Plover. I teach piano."

Karl, who'd been given a pad of lined paper and a pen from Melody Buell, nodded. "Got it."

"Well," Charles began, addressing Sophie, "I believe I heard you refer to our little group as being involved in the Small-Town Olympic *trials*. Or am I mistaken?"

Sophie frowned. "No, that's what I said."

"Well," Charles said again, "as there are only ten of us here to begin with, and the Small-Town Olympics are a friendly, community-based sporting event, it seems counterproductive to hold trials. Aren't we all here to participate?"

Murmured agreement and nodding followed Charles's point.

"It's a competition," Sophie countered. "There's no point of participating in the Olympics if we're not going to give Holliday a run for the money. Our goal is to get attention for Wurst, not to let Jeremy Holliday win *again*."

In the 1800s, Jeremiah Holliday and Seth Wurst, the original founders of both towns, had been best friends, united in their common goal to move West and start a logging town that would welcome people trying to get on their feet financially. However, after a bitter, Romeo-and-Juliet-style rift involving their children, the men split their land into two townships. Holliday thrived; Wurst did not, which was pretty much how things stood today. Eden, who worked for Jeremy Holliday and curated the local history museum, knew the details better than Nikki did.

As for the feud, it had been largely dormant until Sophie Wurst and Jeremy Holliday attended school together, and then KA-BOOM! It had exploded all over again. So much so, in fact, that the two of them were barely able to be civil with each other. Currently, Sophie was expressing her competitive side through the Pacific Northwest Small-Town Olympics, a (supposedly) friendly competition in which teams from towns of no more than twenty-thousand residents gathered to compete in a variety of summer sports.

"Every time Jeremy's team wins," Sophie continued, "he brings in more tourists and more tourist dollars, and Holliday winds up on more Best-Places-To-Visit lists while we languish right next door with our businesses closed and our bank accounts empty." Face flushed beneath her freckles, she pushed back the fringe of curls that nearly covered her eyes. "How many of you are living paycheck to paycheck?"

Hands rose reluctantly around the table.

"We're Social Security check to Social Security check," Leonora Stackler admitted glumly.

"That's right. It's not enough to live on," Mary Anna piped up.

"Exactly. But you two used to run a successful boardinghouse. Am I right?"

Leonora looked embarrassed. Past success highlighted recent struggles. "That was a long time ago," she said quietly.

"Sure was," Mary Anna agreed. "Back when we could afford house repairs and were able to put good food on the table. We lost all our renters, and I doubt anyone would be willing to pay to live in our house now, as broken-down as it is. We can't even afford to sell and move somewhere else."

"You're not going to sell!" Sophie exclaimed. Leveling her most stubborn stare around the table, she said sternly, "No one is going to sell or move. We are going to build Wurst back up to what it used to be."

"A ghost town with a boardinghouse?" Flora muttered, picking at her fingernail polish. Sophie reacted as expected.

"We are not a ghost town! We have never been a ghost town. Seth Wurst intended this community to welcome the stranger and the downtrodden. We were never supposed to be like Holliday, where you're welcomed only for what you can to bring to the city's bank account."

Nikki winced. "I don't know if we can really say that about—"

But Sophie was off and running. While she resentfully enumerated the Hollidays' negative traits

and the others darted angry looks at Flora for pok-
ing the bear with her ghost town comment, Nikki's
thoughts drifted to Drew, who was supposed to have
been on this team with her. One look at him and
Sophie had become delirious with hope. Nikki
hadn't given her the bad news yet.

Someone else was missing from today's meeting: Evan. He lived on the border of Holliday and
Wurst and was a mighty fine athlete. They hadn't
spoken since the night at the bar, where she'd gone
rogue and and kissed him on the lips.

Minn had cornered her at school the next day.

*"What the heck was that about? I thought Anya
was going to stab you with her acrylics. I knew you
and Evan had a thing going!"* She danced around
her desk. *"I called it! Oh, yeah."*

Nikki had assured her friend that she had not
"called it," but rather that Nikki had kissed Evan
to set the stage for their pretend relationship so she
wouldn't have to be "poor Nikki" at the upcoming
weddings, especially her sister's. Minn had said she
understood. (She'd also been disappointed.)

Now all Nikki had to do was convince Evan that
the kiss was simply a set-up for the ruse to come.

She kept watching the door tonight, hoping he
would walk through, yet dreading it, too. Why
had she kissed him—really? Too uncomfortable
to phone him after her moment of madness at the
tavern, she'd been waiting for him to get in touch,

but he hadn't, and every time she thought of Anya, jealousy stirred inside her. The kiss had felt better than she'd intended it to.

That was a problem. Her relationship with Evan had been perfect already. Once they'd confirmed they were friends *only*, they'd been free to call each other anytime, for any reason. The awkwardness between them lately was frustrating. Life was *lonely* without her best male forever (supposed to be forever, anyway) friend.

"Nikki? Nikki!"

Sophie's voice pulled Nikki from her thoughts. When she looked up, everyone at the table was looking at her. "Yes. Uh, here. Present!"

"We're not taking roll." Sophie looked beleaguered. "Drew was supposed to be here to check in about coaching us. We need to set the schedule. Do you have an update from him?"

Oh, crumbs. "Yeah. About that…" She'd had to wheedle and cajole to convince Drew to work with their ragged crew of non-athletes. He considered it negative publicity to coach a team that had no hope of medaling. With their engagement ended, she was positive the possibility of his coaching had ended as well.

"There you are!" Sophie looked to her right as Wurst Burgers's wooden door opened to admit a new arrival. "'Bout time."

"Sorry I'm late, everyone. Childcare issues."

Evan strode to their table, appearing relaxed and comfortable despite his tardiness. Dressed in jeans and a thin V-neck sweater whose pale blue shade matched his eyes and complimented the golden-brown hair that made one think of summer regardless of the time of year, he grabbed a weathered chair from a nearby table and brought it to where Nikki sat.

"Mind if I squeeze in?"

He smiled his typically friendly smile.

All sorts of feelings raced through Nikki's chest and round and round in her head. Relief. Hope. And a sudden, strong yearning that felt like a punch in the solar plexus.

"If there's no room over there, doll face, you can squeeze in next to me." Flora's deep red lips and heavily lashed eyes left no doubt about the welcome he would find.

Nikki saw the amusement sparkle in Evan's gaze and realized how much *she* wanted to be next to him.

"There's plenty of room." The legs of her chair scraped across the floor as she scooted to the right. She looked up at Evan. "Start squeezing."

Chapter Eight

"What'll you have, Evan? I'll fire up the grill." Anthony began to push back his chair to the clear frustration of Sophie, who wanted to get on with business.

"No, thanks. Tony. I grabbed a bite with Noah. I promised him a Wurst burger if he aced his spelling test, though, so we'll see you this weekend."

"He's a great kid, that boy of yours."

"My pride and joy."

Anthony didn't bother to offer Evan a drink. He let his regular customers get their own. Evan didn't seem in a hurry, though, nodding greetings at everyone then settling back in his chair while Sophie brought the meeting to order again.

"What'd I miss?" Evan whispered to Nikki, for his part showing no awkwardness tonight at all.

His physical closeness brought to mind the scene before she'd left the bar—Anya with her arm around him and her cleavage so close to his arm, you couldn't pass a feather between them.

"You didn't miss too much," she whispered back. "Trying to figure out if we should hold tryouts to see who makes the team."

"Say what?"

"Hello? I need your attention up here, *please*." Sophie banged her butter knife on the table again, directing them back to the subject before Evan walked in. "We're planning to have a booth at the Juneeteenth celebration. We're trying to get team sponsors. LeanUp With NorthrUp is our biggest draw, so do we have him confirmed to be there for the day, Nikki?"

Despite the distracting beating of her heart, Nikki caught the rise of Evan's brow.

Nikki knew it was time to disappoint Sophie and the others. Couldn't be helped. She took a deep breath.

"I have some news that may sound upsetting at first. But I know we're smart enough and creative enough to work around it, so it doesn't have to affect the outcome of our endeavors. Although, honestly, isn't the process more important than the end result, anyway?"

Total blank stare response. She cringed a little. Taking another stab at it, she admitted, "Drew and I broke up. He lives in Portland, so he won't be able to participate in the games, according to the rules. It's a shame, but that means the rest of us will just have to take our training more seriously. We are going to be so buff." She gave a half-hearted fist-pump.

"He was going to train us," Flora pointed out.

"Right. But I know a bit about working out. And, Karl, you belong to a gym. We've got this."

"I let that membership lapse," Karl admitted.

"I haven't seen my abs since I got out of the army," Anthony admitted. "This team needs muscle, or we're toast. Gonna look like idiots."

"Okay, everyone, let's take this piece by piece." Evan waded in, his voice calm and friendly, inviting them to change the lens. "First of all, Drew's total-body training relies heavily on a diet featuring cow pancreas and lamb lungs. So, the fact that he won't be with us isn't all bad, am I right?"

Eyes widened and people glanced at each other. Leonora and Mary Anna looked ill. "He's got a point," Mary Anna concurred.

"No, he doesn't." Sophie remained resolute. "LeanUp With NorthrUp is planning to go national. It was in *The Oregonian* Business section. You can't buy this kind of publicity. We could use it for years. We need Drew. Plus, I've already told everyone he's on our team." Her fiery gaze zeroed in on Nikki. "Can you get back together until after the celebration?"

"Sophie!" Melody chastised.

"Man, that's cold." Anthony wagged his head.

"I'm sure there's another way," Mary Anna insisted.

Voices dissented around the table. Sophie shook them off. "Look, emotions are great. We all have 'em. Maybe we even need 'em, I don't know. But they don't have to run the show. We need Northrup."

"Evan's a Northrup," Karl pointed out.

"He's not LeanUp With NorthrUp. He's got no cachet."

Nikki was sure Sophie's pronouncement had no effect on Evan; he'd once told her that having grown up with Steven Northrup, he was immune to rejection. He did not, however, appreciate a demonstrable lack of compassion in anyone, and she felt him reach for her hand beneath the table.

Using a tone of voice that could have halted even eighth-grade defiance in its tracks, Evan stated, "Drew's participation is off the table. Do coaches need to live in city limits?"

Poor Sophie. She wanted so badly to argue, but Evan's tone and expression warned against it.

"No, they don't," Karl responded. "It's in the rule book. 'Coaches, assistant coaches and other ancillary participants as defined in Section 5, paragraph XVII may reside, as their primary residence, outside the boundaries specified for participating athletes.' There's more. Should I continue?"

"No," Sophie said. "We got it."

"Thank you, Karl." Melody smiled sweetly at him.

"Good." Evan nodded. "We have plenty of coaches from the middle and high school to choose from. I'll put the word out. Brandon Buchanan coaches in the community, doesn't he, Nik?"

Brandon was the hulking Scotsman on whom Eden had set her sights prior to falling in love with Gideon. Brandon taught history at the high school and, yes, frequently coached in the community. When she answered affirmatively and said she'd ask if he had the time and interest to help them, Evan looked satisfied.

"Excellent. In the meantime, we'll start working on speed, strength and stamina. I'll help with that as soon as we have a training schedule that can accommodate the majority of us. For anyone who can't attend a training, I'll make a video of the exercises we're going to focus on." He gave Nikki's hand a final squeeze, before pushing back his chair. "You've hardly eaten." He nodded toward the plate in front of her, on which sat a barely touched Wurst burger and cold fries. "Mind if I use your microwave, Tony?" he asked, already picking up her plate.

"'Course not. Get her a new bun. They don't nuke too good."

Mary Anna leaned toward Nikki as Evan walked

to the kitchen. "Isn't it sweet the way he takes care of you? He would have been such a nice brother-in-law."

Leonora nodded. "Very Biblical. 'Her husband's brother shall go in unto her, and take her to him to wife, and perform the duty of a husband's brother unto her.'"

Mary Anna made a face at her sister. "They weren't married yet."

"Who cares?" Flora stroked her décolletage as she gazed dreamily in Evan's direction. "If that boy offered to take care of me, I'd lock it down in a heartbeat."

The men shook their heads and turned their attention to which sports they'd like to try, while Flora and the other women made a couple more comments about the appealing duality of Evan's nurturing qualities and his "rampant masculinity." Melody told Nikki she was terribly sorry about the breakup and said she hoped it wasn't too horribly stressful so close to the wedding.

Fortunately, Sophie's single-mindedness got them back on track. By the time Evan returned with Nikki's burger, Sophie had everyone deeply involved in scheduling.

"That was very nice of you," Nikki whispered as he placed the plate in front of her. "It almost looks like you made me a new one. This looks really good." The meat, veggies and condiments were all stacked perfectly again. "Better than the first time. Don't tell Tony I said that."

"I managed a sandwich shop during grad school."

"That explains why Noah's school lunches look so fantastic."

"Exactly. Eat."

"I'm not all that hungry." Picking up her knife, she divided the hamburger and handed him one half. "Your 'bite' to eat with Noah must have worn off by now." Evan was usually ready for a second meal before Noah went to bed. Wrapping a napkin around his half, she handed it to him.

"You know me well. You sure?"

"Positive."

"Okay. As long as you eat, too."

He seemed prepared to wait, so she picked up her half. Toasting each other with the drippy burgers, they bit in. Nikki clearly heard Mary Anna whisper, "Isn't that darling?"

Winking at Nikki, Evan grinned as he chewed.

Some…energy…rushed through the center of her body, a *zing* that felt almost like an anxiety attack. Or an orgasm. Either this was a really, *really* good burger, or the feeling of being cared for by a man—by Evan—coupled with the warmth of people smiling at them, was making her yearn.

This was what Eden had with Gideon, this… nurturing thing. Evan was good at it. It probably came from being a dad.

Had he been nurturing with Anya after Nikki left the bar?

Clearly the *zing* had not come from the hamburger, because the food very quickly turned to something tasteless and rubbery. Swallowing it gave her a stomachache.

As Sophie conducted a survey of optimal times to train, the door to Wurst Burgers opened again, admitting a family of two adults, two young children and a baby in a blue-and-purple woven sling the woman wore around her body. The man held his hand affectionately on top of the head of a boy who appeared to be a couple of years older than Noah. A dainty girl clung to her mother's hand.

"Matteo, *Como estas*, amigo?" Tony rose from his chair, greeting the man by name. *"Es esta su familia?"*

"Si." The man, Matteo, nodded proudly when Tony asked if this was his family. *"Mi esposa*, Martina. *Mi hijo*, Sebastian. *El bebé*, Eduardo." He nodded toward the perfect little girl. *"Y etse chica linda es mi hija* Jenni. *Hoy es su cumpleaños."*

Nikki listened avidly to the conversation. Everyone she met expected her to speak Spanish, simply based on her appearance. In truth, even though she'd lived in the US from the time she was six months old, Spanish had turned out to be one of her toughest subjects in school. She'd repeated Spanish Three twice. Tony, who was Italian, seemed more in fluent in Spanish than she. Still, she understood enough to know it was the beautiful little girl's birthday. The mother beamed with pride. Even the child's older brother grinned.

"We get to eat out on birthdays!" he piped up in English, making the others laugh.

"Birthdays are special," Tony agreed. "How old are you?" He bent down to the little girl, who raised five fingers, simultaneously showing a row of perfect tiny teeth.

"Holy cow, this must be your lucky day." Tony slapped his thigh. "Tonight, we're giving free milkshakes to five-year-olds. And their brothers."

Jenni's dark brown eyes got huge. She looked around the restaurant as if to see whether the other diners heard this amazing news, and her gaze locked with Nikki's.

Nikki smiled at her. They had the same café-au-lait skin and black hair, though Jenni wore two neat braids revealing tiny flower earrings, and Nikki's hair was wound into a messy bun. Jenni also had on a necklace, pink skirt and matching sweater under which peeked a T-shirt bearing the image of a Disney princess.

She was exactly the way Nikki had pictured a daughter of her own.

Pain filled her chest—a literal, physical ache. Her wedding would have taken place in a few short weeks. She'd turn thirty-seven the week after that, on what was supposed to have been a quick weekend honey-moon getaway, followed by a longer lovers' vacay when both she and Drew could stay away longer. Summers were his busiest season.

So many plans. So very many plans that had made thirty-seven feel like the start of something, not the end. But now...

Ovaries didn't do their job forever; if hers decided to take early retirement, then the dream of a family she was related to by blood and flesh and bone would be gone.

It shouldn't matter. You're adopted. You know love is more than DNA.

Maybe she'd be in her forties by the time she and the right guy found each other. Maybe her fifties? *(Dear God, please not that long.)* Maybe she wouldn't have a biological family of her own. *It shouldn't matter.*

It mattered.

"Do you believe in arranged marriages?"

The whispered question came from her left. Like her, Evan was watching Jenni, the birthday girl, as her mother and father continued to chat with Tony before they sat down.

Evan's question did nothing to slow the racing of her heart. Nor did the fact that he reached for her hand again.

Turning toward Nikki, he grinned. "I think I found Noah's future bride." As he looked into her eyes, he must have noted she was starting to panic. The fingers around hers tightened as his features drew together in concern. "Nik? What's wrong?"

My life. Seriously. My freaking solo life.

Surrounded by family, surrounded by community and by kids and coworkers all day long, she was still alone. Even here, with Evan holding her hand and looking into her eyes, she was a single person on the road to living alone, no kids of her own, and she was almost forty. It seemed now that she's been looking for connection all her life. Looking in all the wrong places.

Pulling her fingers from his, she fumbled for her purse and stood. "I have to go."

Sophie looked up from the other end of the table. "Where are you going? What's your schedule? We need to nail this—"

"I have another appointment." With a whopper of an anxiety attack. "I'll call you."

She hurried out the door, trying not to make eye contact with the little girl, but her gaze was drawn like a magnet. *I hope you find your prince... Or your princess... Or whoever you want that makes you feel alive. Someday, little Jenni. Don't settle for anything less than love.*

As if she heard Nikki's thoughts, Jenni turned, and the sweetness of her smile filled Nikki with a yearning that hurt like hell.

She was practically hyperventilating by the time

she reached her car. Firm hands turned her around as she fumbled in her purse for her key fob, clumsy with panic and emotion.

"What's wrong?" Evan asked her again, blue eyes dark and piercing with concern.

For starters, I don't think I ever loved your brother.

The realization had hit her with gale force in the restaurant. Now it seemed to fill every cell.

For as long as she could remember, she had found herself wanting, lacking something she couldn't name, as if life was a grand party that looked incredibly fun, but she wasn't invited. Being with Drew had made her feel as if she'd finally received an invitation to the hottest party on the block.

That sounded frighteningly immature. Her self-image had always been a little off. In grad school, she'd had a therapist named Sue, who'd told her she had impostor syndrome: Anytime she'd felt successful, she'd been sure someone was going to out her as a fraud.

Tears felt like fire at the backs of her eyes. She'd felt elated and bubbly and giddy at various times with Drew, but she'd never been serene. How could she? Always trying to lose body fat, pump more weights, avoid another carb—deep down, hadn't she been afraid the entire time that he was going to leave? Yes. Yes, she had.

Now she had to wonder: Did she even know what romantic *love* felt like?

Hard to believe that after almost four decades of life and a degree in psychology, she was asking that question?

The feeling of defeat was exhausting. Pretending to be okay felt exhausting. "I'm almost thirty-seven," she answered Evan, "I'm not sure I've ever been in love. That's incredibly sad, don't you think?"

Aw, hell.

Look anywhere, Evan ordered himself, *anywhere but at her lips.*

Because, among other reasons, a man's first response to "I'm not sure I've ever been in love" should not be *I really want to get naked with you*.

Right? Or was there some leeway here? Because if the jury was still out...

No, no, the jury was not out. It was wrong. He needed to reboot.

Not for the first time lately, Evan didn't know how to handle a moment with Nikki. *Did* he think there was something terribly sad about her not knowing if she'd ever been in love? Not really. He didn't know, either.

"What's love?" he asked her, hearing a tinge of cynicism in his voice. "People throw the word around like it's *hello*. You made me watch *The Bachelor* with you, so I know you know what I'm talking about. Thinking you feel it doesn't mean it's going to last."

"Yes. But I also know what I want."

"What do you want?"

Nikki's huge brown eyes, so dark they looked black in all but the brightest lighting, scanned the wide-open field across from the restaurant. She wasn't wearing much makeup today, but her lashes were so damn long and naturally as black as her hair, it looked as if she wore false eyelashes all the time.

The roundness of her face had always bothered her, but he liked it. Her cheeks pushed up when she smiled, and her chin was distinct and softly pointed like a cat's, with a faint cleft he found himself looking for right now. She didn't like her lips, either—too big, she said, which was BS from any man's point of view. It may have been only one night, but he still remembered what it felt like to press his own lips to a generous mouth like that, and…yeah, definitely not too big. In fact, he'd like to—

"I want to belong to someone forever. In a way that can't be broken."

Damn. All right, he needed to keep his friendship cap on. He could do that.

Nikki's voice was soft, her eyes too bright in the way that signaled tears. That wasn't good. A young child's tears, Evan had learned to handle; a woman's, he had not.

"You do belong to people. You've got a family that would do anything for you," he said, too emphatically, breaking the number one rule in the cornucopia of parenting classes he had taken when he'd found out he was going to be a father: *When someone is upset, validate, don't educate.*

Nikki's well-shaped brows puckered. Her full lips pressed together, and her expression seemed to close up, no longer vulnerable.

And that, schmuck, is why you don't try to talk people out of what they're feeling.

Guilt socked him in the gut. He hated what the breakup with his deep-as-an-oil-slick brother was doing to her. "This is why I stick to the one-month-maximum rule." When she frowned, he explained, "No dating the same person for longer than a month. I've told you that."

"No, you didn't. I'd have remembered that."

"Hey!" Sophie called from the restaurant entrance. "If you two are staying, I need your schedules!"

"C'mon." Swiftly, Evan grabbed Nikki's arm and hustled her toward the dirt path alongside the road. There were enough trees to make it a shady, pleasant walk to the center of "downtown," which in Wurst described a collection of brick-and-wood buildings that should have been bulldozed a couple decades ago.

"Don't look back. Just keep walking," he instructed, ignoring Sophie's exasperated voice as she reminded them loudly that "There's no success without commitment!"

"We'll have to go back to get our cars eventually," Nikki reminded him.

"Maybe she'll be gone by then." When he realized he was still holding on to her arm halfway to town, Evan released her. He'd walked by Nikki's side numerous times—through Doc Shlessinger Park in Holliday; along Northwest Twenty-Third in Portland while she checked out the stores and he and Noah scoped out the best places for dessert; shuffling through the leaves on Holliday's Liberty Street for the Halloween costume parade. Talk and laughter had always come effortlessly to them. In fact, his relationship with Nikki was the easiest he'd ever had.

Except for the hours immediately after they'd had sex. And right now.

"About a one-month-maximum rule," she said. "Does that apply to every woman? Even if you two really get along?"

"I'm sure we've talked about this."

"I'm positive we haven't. I'd have remembered."

They walked silently for several paces. The town was quiet and still on a Saturday evening. Then again, Wurst was always quiet and still unless Sophie cooked up trouble.

"So when you and I slept together," she ventured,

and every muscle in Evan's body clenched, "the longest we ever would have dated is one month?"

Were fire-red ants crawling up his body right now? It felt as if fire ants were crawling up his body. "I don't know. Maybe. I suppose." That was not how he'd felt on the night in question, however. Or the morning after. "I didn't think about it."

"Why not?"

Exasperated, Evan stopped and turned toward her. "I don't know. Probably because you jumped out of bed like it was about to blow up and mumbled some nonsense about wasn't-that-great-let's-never-do-it-again."

"I didn't mumble." Nikki did what she always did when confronted: she rose on the balls of her feet as if trying to add height to her petite frame. It seemed unconscious; he'd always thought it was adorable. "I spoke very clearly, thank you. We were friends, and you have never been available for long term—although until today I didn't realize one month was your shelf life—and I did want long term, which I have always been clear about, so the two of us having sex was…"

She couldn't find the word.

"Complicated," he supplied.

"*Very* complicated. Yes. Hazardous to the friendship," she added.

"And to you personally."

She blinked, surprised. "No."

"Yes. You could have fallen in love with me."

Nikki looked almost affronted. "I didn't. I wouldn't have."

Evan felt a smile pull on his lips. Don't ask him why he was suddenly enjoying this, but he was. "Yeah, you would have. Best friends," he pointed out before she had a chance to rebut, "great sex—it's a recipe for infatuation at the very least."

"Using that logic, you would have fallen in love with me, too."

"Or been infatuated."

"At the very least."

Their eyes were locked, and he knew they were both so stubborn that neither would be willing to be the first to look away. Lavender twilight made Wurst a little lovelier than it was in full daytime. A sweet breeze lifted strands of black hair that escaped from Nikki's messy bun. She'd decided to get bangs a few months ago, instantly regretted it and had been growing them out ever since. Sometimes, when she was concentrating, she'd pull on them as if trying to stretch them out. He liked that he knew that about her.

"I like being your friend." He said the words aloud but wasn't sure he'd meant to. It was a sort of preface for the thought that followed: *I think we would have liked being lovers* and *friends*.

"Good thing I said what I did then," Nikki murmured. "Two years ago, I wanted a ring and a wedding date. And a registry at Babies R Us."

Reaching out, he tucked the flyaway strands of hair behind her ear. Shouldn't have, but did. "And now all you want is to belong to someone forever."

She nodded. "Yeah. I'm needy that way."

He hadn't grown up with the best examples of healthy relationships or of emotional health in general. Maybe that was why he couldn't identify what he was feeling at this moment. Physically, it didn't feel good—this tight, hot, burning sensation in his chest and gut, as if there was a battle roaring inside.

"C'mon, let's keep walking," she said, tugging his upper arm. And, once they were in step again, she admitted, "I think Eden's pregnant. She hasn't said so, but that's probably because she doesn't want me to feel sad. She canceled brunch today because she wasn't feeling well, and last week she turned down a mimosa and had her hand on her stomach under the table. And I wanted to ask her and to celebrate with her—I know how much she wants a family and how worried she was that it might never happen—but I was afraid I'd cry for the wrong reasons. I'm a terrible friend." Her voice shook slightly.

"You are not a terrible friend. I speak from experience." The desire to take her in his arms, to ease her pain, made the battle inside more explosive. He didn't trust himself to hug her; friend or no friend, he was still a guy, and he was…feeling some things.

"I like that you have a one-month dating rule," she said.

Where the hell had that come from? "You do?"

She nodded, hands in the pockets of a fuchsia cardigan she wore over skinny jeans and a tight-fitting black top with a neckline low enough for him to see the top of her cleavage, which, thanks be to God, was still freaking gorgeous despite her weight loss.

Her face was forward, her expression focused. "The good thing about our dating each other is that it's time limited. Knowing that right up front is very relaxing, isn't it?"

He felt his muscles tense. "Very."

Nikki's expression was impersonal, almost businesslike. "I need to attend three weddings before July. The first one is Eden's brother's; I'm only a guest at that one. Then there's my sister's wedding." Her brows dipped further. "Obviously that will be the toughest. Then a few weeks later, I'm Eden's maid of honor. Of course, if I can get through Gia's wedding, Eden's ought to be a piece of cake." Her expression became determinedly spunky. "Get it? Wedding cake? Ba-da-bum. I really appreciate that you're willing to pretend to be my date. My mother calls me every day to do a depression checklist. You were right—if everyone thinks we're dating, it'll be much easier."

He grinned. "I'm usually right."

"Don't ruin it. As for the one-month shelf life on dating, I can tell everyone I knew that ahead of time and was all for it."

"Whoa. You're going to tell people?"

Nikki nodded vigorously. "Well, yeah. I think I should, don't you? It'll keep them from hating you."

"Hating me?"

"For dumping me after the weddings."

"Maybe they'll think you dumped me."

"Possibly. But then they'll think I'm an idiot. You're considered quite a catch."

"Good to know. So you want people to believe we both agreed from the outset that this would be a temporary arrangement."

"Very temporary. Only long enough to decide whether we were compatible as lovers and once we realized we weren't—"

"Wait a minute. You want people to believe we're not compatible in bed?"

"I've thought about it, and it's our best bet. You already convinced Gia we had sex. So, we need to tell them we tried, it didn't really mesh and we decided we're better off as friends."

"That's a problem."

"Why?"

"You said it yourself: I'm a catch. I have a reputation. No one is going to believe *I* didn't satisfy *you* in bed. So…" He shrugged, looking at her meaningfully.

Her dark eyes widened adorably when she realized the implication. "You want people to think *I'm* bad in bed?"

"Not 'bad.' Just not…satisfying. Like you said." Evan had to struggle to maintain a straight face.

"I did not say— Okay look, that is wrong on so many levels." Nikki gave him her most ferocious shame-on-you scowl. "We're fake dating to comfort my family and save my dignity, not blast it to smithereens."

"Sorry."

"Also, I am not bad in bed." Her eyes narrowed as a new, obviously offending thought occurred. "Did you think I was bad in bed?"

For crying out loud. He was tempted to show her how very *not* bad in bed he thought she was. When she'd kissed him the other night, a flood of memory had filled him. The truth was that night with her two years ago had been different from every other night he'd shared with a woman. He hadn't been able to get enough of her, had felt as if he'd never be able to get enough of her. It had been exhilarating, intoxicating. Frightening as hell.

When she'd acted as though it was a foregone conclusion they'd return to being friends only, he hadn't known whether to punch something in frustration or sigh in relief.

"I did not think you were bad in bed," he said matter-of-factly in the understatement of the century. "In fact, I think we can both agree the sex was fantastic. So fantastic," he lowered his voice, taking a step closer, "that we may be in very great danger."

Swallowing visibly, Nikki rasped, "What kind of danger?"

"We could ruin our friendship if one of us becomes attracted to the other while we're pretending. Is that a risk you want to take?"

"Oh. Well… I don't think… I mean, *maybe* that could happen. Maybe, but…" She looked as if she'd run too far too fast. "What do you want to do about it?"

"It's obvious, isn't it? We've got to kiss."

Chapter Nine

Spring evenings in the mid-Willamette Valley were cool bordering on chilly, but Nikki felt like ripping off her sweater. Perspiration gathered between her breasts.

Other than their one wild, unprecedented and never-repeated night, he hadn't behaved suggestively with her. Hadn't flirted. Did not blur the lines.

This evening? Very blurry.

It was a bit weird to have this conversation in the middle of the street, even a street as quiet as this one.

Anytime she looked at Evan, she thought he was handsome, but tonight he seemed to ooze sex appeal.

Waiting for her response, he tilted his head.

"Feelings come up. You know?" he said. "Feelings that can overwhelm reason. I can't take that responsibility anymore. Assuming you're…neutral…after the kiss, I'll still be happy to be your date."

She stopped breathing for a moment. "Wait. Are you for real?" Nikki turned to scrutinize his face in the deepening light. He didn't look like he was kidding. He really didn't. "You're worried about *me* losing control. Not you. Me." Pressing her fingers to her temples, she said, "Oh. My. Holy. Heaven. The ego!"

"Yep. Genetic defect. Let's hope it skips a generation this time, right? Okay, you ready?"

"What? No." She slapped his arm as he leaned toward her. "Have you lost your mind? I'm not going to kiss you to see if I get 'feelings.' That's ridiculous. We've already had sex."

"Shh." He indicated their surroundings. "Please, I try to keep my private life private." He took a step forward and spoke softly. "Nikki, you and I didn't kiss when we had sex."

"I beg your freaking pardon? We certainly did."

"No. Think back. We never kissed on the lips. I kissed your neck." His gaze fell purposefully to her décolletage. "And…" he pointed "…right there. A few other places." He glanced lower, and even though she was thoroughly clothed, she suddenly felt naked. Memories of that night lit up her brain and her body. "And you kissed me…" Without naming body parts, he put a hand on his flat belly, re-membering. "But definitely," he emphasized, his eyes meeting hers and darkening to sexy, sultry cobalt, "definitely not on the lips."

Dear Lord. She had never felt so turned on in her life. Chance of remaining neutral if she kissed him right now? Snowball, welcome to hell.

"We kissed on the lips at Leo's. I won't speak for you, but I didn't feel anything." *Oooh, liar.*

Nikki saw a glint of amusement in Evan's re-markable gaze. "The peck you gave me? You call that a kiss?" He wagged his head. "Honey, even as your fake date, I'm going to do a *lot* better than that. See, now I know for sure that we need a test run. I don't want to break up after the weddings and leave you pining for something you'll never have again. It wouldn't be fair to you."

He was baiting her, tossing down the glove, and a responding excited energy coursed through her. *Two could play that game.*

She squared her shoulders, refusing to be intimi-dated. "You're not worried about me. You're afraid *you* can't stand the heat. And I get it, Evan. You're so used to keeping things superficial." Taking a step toward him, Nikki kept her gaze locked with his. "It makes sense that you're afraid of what might happen when you're with someone real." She took another step closer and laid a hand on his chest. "Someone substantial. You might feel…too much." She lowered her voice, almost to a whisper. "It's scary." Her shoulders rose in a small shrug. "Fine. Kiss me."

More often than not, Evan was able to school his features to an affable charm. Not now. He seemed off-kilter. Unsure of exactly how to respond. When a car drove past, he glanced around. A lot of people in town knew them both; Evan and Nikki took care of their teens. If they kissed out in the open and someone saw them, rumors would swirl like leaves in autumn.

Suddenly, the corners of his mouth rose slightly. He still expected her to back down. "Right here?" he asked, indicating the street.

"No," she responded, pointing to her lips. "Right here."

The sun had nearly set, but they were close enough for her to see him clearly, and if anyone thought blue eyes weren't warm, they hadn't been touched by the fire in Evan's.

Nikki's heart raced as he took a step toward her this time. Not moving was one of the hardest things she'd ever done as he slid one hand around the nape of her neck, cupping her jaw with the other, his palms big and warm.

No kiss had ever taken so long to consummate. Or maybe it only felt that way to Nikki because every nerve ending in her body was electrified with desire.

Heat radiated from both their bodies; she could feel it. His lips came closer…and closer…

What are you waiting for! Her mind shouted the demand as desire coursed through her body. And then—

The hell with it.

She closed the distance between them herself, re-alizing exactly what he'd been waiting for—the mo-ment of explosive, cataclysmic *surrender* that came after intense anticipation. The hunger she felt as she wound her arms around him beat anything she'd felt while going through the motions of romance with Drew. *This* felt like being fed after starving for most of her life.

The first kiss was an appetizer, a tease that Evan controlled as he held her head and kissed her softly…once…twice…before tracing the shape of her lips with his tongue.

Nikki delved her fingers into the thick waves of hair at the nape of his neck and gave herself com-pletely to the moment. When he felt her lean into him, Evan moved to the main course—a kiss that both fed and devoured. The scent of him, warm and clean and beachy, had always been a pleasing comfort. Now it intoxicated, filling her senses and driving out every thought.

And summer was coming up.

She wanted to press her body to his, to feel that solid chest against hers, but the way he was holding her face kept some space between them, adding a stronger yearning and sexual frustration to the waves of pure sensation crashing inside her. Awareness of time and space fled entirely.

As slowly as the kiss had begun and as powerfully as it built, that's how swiftly Evan brought it to an end.

He took a step back. Then he lowered his hands.

Abruptly, Nikki let her arms fall to her sides and opened her eyes. The sun had set more while they were kissing, and she was glad. Her face was burning hot. The last time she was this breathless, she'd just finished a HIIT workout with Drew. Evan's chest rose and fell, too.

"So," he said, clearing his throat. "We're good then?"

It took her a moment to realize what he meant.

She blinked. "Yeah," she agreed. "We're good. *I'm* good. Still friend-zoning over here. You?"

In the lavender light, she saw him nod. "No surprises."

"All right. Great." They stood in fraught-with-tension silence until she hitched a thumb over her shoulder. "I'm going to get my car."

He nodded. "I'm going to walk a little more… unless you want me to walk you back?"

Ordinarily he wouldn't ask; he never let her walk alone, even in an area as safe as theirs.

"Nope. I'm good." She needed to get home, into

her own space, into her own head. She needed to think, not feel, never mind that she was a counselor. Beginning to turn in the direction from which they'd just come, she paused. "Oh hey, would you tell Noah I said yes."

"Yes?"

"To Special Person's Day. He left a voice mail asking if I could go."

"He did?"

She nodded. "Are you okay with that?"

Evan hesitated a moment, but answered, "Of course. My son is making his own social calendar now. I need to get used to him growing up."

They smiled over their shared appreciation for Noah then slipped again into awkward quiet.

"Well, 'night." Nikki offered a brief wave that Evan returned. Then they stood where they were, staring at each other through the gathering dark. This was the time to be rational, intellectual, wise.

There was nothing more to say, so she turned and began to walk, aware that her legs felt as flaccid as her brain. And, maybe it was her imagination…probably it was her imagination…but it felt as if Evan was still watching her. Her back burned.

Ignoring the sensation, she kept moving, head up as if she didn't have a care, definitely not lusting after her ex-fiance's brother-slash-best male forever friend. This was another fine mess she'd gotten herself into.

* * *

Move. Get going. You've got a kid at home.

Wurst was freakishly safe, even at night, plus Nikki knew Krav Maga and was a volunteer instructor for GirlStrength; there was no need to continue watching her.

Converse high tops added no height to her petite frame, nor did they contribute to the hypnotic sway of her hips, though sway her hips certainly did. Drew had never appreciated Nikki's sensuality.

And you shouldn't, either.

Forcing himself to turn around, Evan walked, trying to release some energy before he went back for his own car. Why had he pushed Nikki to kiss?

Ego. Lust. Usually he could rely on reason, or at the very least fear and caution, to control his damned self. Instead, he'd teased her and taunted, daring her to prove she wouldn't be affected if he kissed her the way he'd been yearning to almost for as long as they'd known each other.

Had she been unaffected? *No.* No, he'd felt her body quiver. The satisfaction was stronger than any drug.

He'd waited a long time for confirmation that she'd been more affected by their lovemaking than she'd been willing to admit two years ago. Back then, she'd pulled away from him and moved on with Drew so quickly that he'd wondered if their night had meant anything at all. After the disaster of his marriage, he'd been plain afraid to pursue Nikki. Afraid to hurt her, himself and his son. Better off friends. Except now...

Now the satisfaction he felt from their kiss was as much of an aphrodisiac as the kiss itself.

They were going to pretend to be a couple for her sake.

She'd hang out with Noah for his son's sake.

Would he be able to keep his hands off her, for heaven's sake?

Doc Schlessinger Park, on the easternmost end of Holliday, occupied fifteen acres of wetlands punctuated by a meandering boardwalk, plus another thirty acres of jogging trail, splash pad, gazebo, playground, dog park and sports field. For a town of fewer than eight thousand residents, the park was the jewel in their crown.

"Who put the circuit stations in?" Minn panted as she and Nikki paused during their jog to do fifteen jump squats.

"Not sure."

"I'm dying."

"No, you're not." Leaping from the squat position to standing straight then back to a squat, Nikki was pleased to see she hadn't lost much strength even though she hadn't exercised since before her broken engagement. Stamina was another issue. They'd been jogging around the trail only ten minutes and, honestly, she'd just as soon break for lunch as do another lap. Too much sugar and sitting on her couch, contemplating her future, were making her soft in more ways than one. "Keep going. Remember, you said you wanted to exercise one minute for every year of your age."

"I didn't mean it. I was drunk."

"You were not drunk."

"I should have been. It's the only thing that would explain why I agreed to self-torture." Minn's squats were becoming higher and her jumps lower. Her arms flopped at her sides. "It's Sunday brunchtime. We should be lifting mimosas, not using up every last bit of cartilage in our knees."

"Do your knees hurt?" Nikki asked with concern. Minn was twelve, almost thirteen years older than she was.

"If I say yes, can we walk the rest of the way?"

After squat fifteen, Nikki put her hands on her hips, took a belly breath and blew it out. "Sure. Fine." Whom was she trying to impress, anyway?

This morning, she'd put on a sports bra, cropped tee and leggings in a deep fuchsia that screamed "Go ahead and look." Last time she'd had this outfit on, however, her abs had been flat with visible muscle. Today she had a food baby. With her hands still on her hips, she bent forward to stretch her hamstrings. Her hip bones, too, had a layer of padding she hadn't seen in a while. Couldn't blame her split from Drew for that; she'd been carbo loading on Saturdays for a few months. Her family was Jewish, for crying out loud. She'd grown up with bagels and challah French toast and *matzah brei* on Saturday mornings. Better still had been the raucous conversation between her and her siblings, her mother's famous care packages filled with food and love, her father's endless search for the perfect blender... She'd drifted away from the family fold for a time, spending her Saturdays with Drew or Eden instead. Now, with Drew out of the picture completely and Eden building a new life with Gideon, she was enjoying the family, realizing how much she'd missed the sense of tradition and togetherness.

"Let's walk," she said, waving them both forward as they resumed progress along the path. "I'll get more steps in later, anyway. I'm going to the mall to look for a ring for Gia's 'Something Blue.' I'm thinking aquamarine."

"I still can't believe you gave her your wedding day. Why torture yourself?"

"I'm not torturing myself. It'll be fine." Hopefully. With Evan.

As they strolled, Nikki breathed in the soothing quiet of a Sunday in the park. Not too many people were out and about yet but come Memorial Day there would be noise and action. Being part of a community where people knew each other had been a true perk of her job here in Holliday.

"I slept with Leo." Minn's announcement came out of the blue, causing such a shockwave through her walking partner that Nikki missed a tree root pushing up a section of the path and tripped, taking a few steps before she caught herself.

"Sheesh, Minn, I could use a little prelude next time, okay? Leo? Leo's Tavern Leo?"

"Yes."

"And by 'slept with,' you mean…"

"We did the nasty on his couch. And then his bed."

"Okay." She had to process that. The principal of her school, who possessed a doctorate in Education, season tickets to the Portland Opera and a wardrobe that consisted mainly of conversative suits with below-the-knee skirts, had gone all the way with Leo. Nikki didn't even know the Leo's last name; because he never even seemed to socialize outside of his work. "Do you know his last name?" she asked. "I'm not judging. I just realized I don't know it."

"No. I forgot to ask."

At forty-nine, Minn possessed the bold redheaded look of her Irish family with fair skin, classic features and a smattering of freckles. She had been married for over twenty years until very recently Her husband, Scott…soon to be her *ex*-husband Scott…was a law professor at Willamette U. He had cheated on her with a Doctor of Jurisprudence candidate he called "the woman I've been waiting for." Minn hadn't known her husband had been waiting for someone else.

"So are you and Leo dating?"

"No. It was a one-night thing."

Like her "thing" with Evan? Minn's auburn brows pulled together in thought. She used to be a dynamo, her energy seeming boundless and vibrant. Since the divorce…and now her thing with Leo…she appeared unsettled, questioning herself and life in general.

"Love was supposed to make life easier," Nikki murmured, wondering if she should have kept the thought to herself, but Minn looked over and immediately nodded.

"Right. Or if not easier, more comforting. Like having a soft bed to fall into at the end of a hard day. My bed feels like a giant brick. Love makes everything harder once you've been betrayed." She took a deep breath in, before releasing it with a weary sigh. "How do you trust again?"

As if the heavens heard Minn's question, a voice called out from behind them, "Hey! Nik! Minn!"

They turned to find Eden Berman-Soon-To-Be-Bowen and her fiancé, Gideon, about thirty feet behind. Waiting while the couple jogged up, Nikki felt a pinch in her chest as she took in her college friend's face—devoid of its usual artful makeup application. Eden wore her thick hair in a simple high pony, and her clothes were just what you'd expect for a Sunday walk in the park instead of her previous elaborate vintage or overtly sexy outfits. Gideon, the most unlikely man on the planet, had become Eden's soft bed.

Eden hugged Nikki first, then tossed an arm around Minn's shoulders and gave her a squeeze, too. "Minnie, I'll see you at book group tomorrow night, right? I really want to hear your take on *Faye, Faraway*."

"Oh." Minn looked a bit sheepish. "I didn't read it." The principal didn't do her homework. So unlike her.

"That's fine. Come for the snacks, okay?"

In her own happiness over finding her *bashert*, the love she believed was meant-to-be, Eden was committed to taking emotional care of her two friends who had recently suffered the old dump-ola. She'd been there once herself.

Minn shrugged, her shoulders uncharacteristically hunched. "Sure."

Gideon looked at Nikki. "Are you jogging today? How's the ankle?"

A few months ago, she'd pulled a ligament while working out with Drew. She'd seen her best friend's fiancé, their trusty hometown doctor, who had sent her for X-rays and advised her on care.

"It's good. No lasting issues. I'm not working out as hard as I used to, anyway." She hadn't intended to say that, hadn't made the decision until this moment. But it was certainly accurate. "It was taking over my life. And my body. I'm not really the rock-hard-abs type."

Eden's eyes grew wide. She'd been talking to Nikki about the manic exercise and restrictive diet for months. Her smile held a world of love and approval.

When was the last time I looked at me that way? Nikki wondered. And why was it so damn hard?

"Can you get together next week to talk about your bridal shower?" Nikki asked, instantly seeing the hesitation in her friend's eyes.

"Yeah, about the bridal shower… I'm not really the bridal shower type—"

"Do not start with me." Nikki preempted any effort on Eden's part to diminish her own wedding experience. "Gideon, please tell your lovely fiancée that every bride-to-be needs a bridal shower. Also, that I am doing great and do not need her to protect me."

In an uncharacteristic moment of PDA, Gideon hugged his bride-to-be and murmured against her temple, "You definitely need a party. Also, Nikki does not need you to protect her. This time." He tilted his head at Nikki. "We all need it sometimes."

As Nikki's maid of honor, Eden had already thrown Nikki a perfect bridal shower at the Moonstone Spa in Silverton, Oregon. They'd had it on the books for months. Preparations for Eden's wedding, on the other hand, had begun only weeks ago. Nikki had been over the moon to return the favor of being a maid of honor…although with Eden and Gideon's wedding taking place after hers, she'd expected to be a *matron* of honor.

"Nothing elaborate," Eden reminded Nikki now. "Low-key and simple with just a couple of people."

"Hardly any people, hardly any decorations, easy on the fun. Got it." Nikki nodded. "It'll be so great!"

"Hilarious."

"My new plan is to ignore you and take the ball into my own hands." Nikki was about to mention a venue when a loud, joyful voice called her name.

"Aunt Nikki! Aunt Nikki!"

"Noah! Come back here!"

Eden and Gideon, Minn and Nikki turned toward the raised voices to see Noah tearing across the grassy field from the direction of the play structure. His arms and legs pumped as he ignored his father, who jogged behind him.

The six-year-old used the lower half of Nikki's body to stop his momentum. "I saw you from way over there." He pointed happily then wrapped his arms around her hips.

Nikki melted even as Evan stopped in front of them, hands on his hips as he caught his breath and frowned mightily at his son. "When I say stop, that is a red light, buddy. A red light. This is a *safety issue*. Is that clear?"

"Yes, Dad." Nikki felt Noah sigh against her leg. He looked up at her. "We're gonna eat pancakes. Can you eat with us?"

Nikki met Evan's eyes. When she hesitated, he looked at the others. "Sorry for the interruption. Gideon, Eden, good to see you." The men shook hands. "Minn, you haven't seen Noah since he was a toddler, have you?"

"No." The high school principal smiled at the boy. "I like pancakes with bananas and chocolate chips. And a scoop of ice cream."

Noah's eyes popped.

"We've been talking about planning Eden's bridal shower," Nikki said. "Maybe that's what we should serve."

"Actually, we were talking about keeping it as simple as possible," Eden put in. "Or not having one at all, because I'm really not a bridal shower person."

With one hand on Noah's head and the other on her hip, Nikki said, "Eden is still trying to protect me. She thinks I'm going to fall apart if I see someone else happy in a love."

"That isn't it at all," Eden protested.

"Hey, bud," Evan said to Noah. "The bucket swing is free. Run over and grab it. I'll be right over to push you."

"Will you do an underdog?"

"The best one you've ever seen."

With a whoop, Noah took off, shouting, "Bye, Aunt Nikki!" as he ran.

As soon as his son was out of earshot, Evan assured Eden, "Nik's not going to fall apart. Why would she?" Moving to her side, he slid an arm around her waist. "I can't say for sure that she's in love with me—yet—but I am definitely committed to keeping her happy." He glanced down, the look he gave her so smoldering it could set the entire park ablaze.

She giggled involuntarily, due as much to goose bumps as to nerves. Minn, who knew the truth, arched a brow. Eden, who did not know the truth, also arched a brow.

When they'd agreed to go forward with the ruse, she'd somehow thought she would be in control of the situation, deciding when and how to, well, basically lie to her friends and family. (With their own good in mind, of course.)

Glad for Evan's arm around her as her legs were beginning to shake, she said, "Sure. Let's tell them everything…" It seemed she should use an endearment, so she added the first one that came to mind. "Snookums."

Evan's expression changed, but subtly so that only she would notice it. *You're not calling me that.*

Sorry. I suck at improv. Which he should know, having played Rumor Has It with her numerous times. Her stories never sounded believable. Looking up at him, she smiled, trying to look besotted. "You start."

Chapter Ten

Cinco de Mayo was one of Holliday, Oregon's most colorful and musically rich celebrations. Felipa Ramos and her daughter Valentina, from Thanksgiving, the local diner, served hot hand-made tortillas, stuffed plantains and *chuchitos*, the delicious round tamales from their native Guatemala. Nikki's mother and father had gifted her with a family trip to Guatemala for her thirteenth birthday. Having left the country of her birth while still in her infancy, the languages, sights, scents and cuisine had been as foreign to her as they had been to the rest of her USA- and Korean-born family. She'd loved it, though, which had whetted her appetite to learn more about her culture. Moving to Holliday and meeting the Ramoses had been a great gift. Felipa had taught her to make *pepian*, a curry-like stew with sesame and pumpkin seeds, and Valentina had introduced her to the tradition of hand-embroidered textiles.

Mexican traditions abounded in Holliday, too. Cinco de Mayo was one celebration during which their next-door neighbors in Wurst were fully involved or had been until the surge in immigration detention in 2017. Since then, many of their compatriots had kept to themselves or moved from the area entirely, in some cases relinquishing businesses it had taken years to build. To Nikki, that was a tragic reminder that the American dream was a relative experience. She was the first person in her birth family to have graduated high school, yet the privilege of education was hers because she'd been adopted. She hadn't had to risk her life to be here or to stay here.

As the absence of their immigrant neighbors became more pronounced, Nikki answered the call the local Hispanic community put out to keep the Cinco de Mayo celebration alive, which is how she found herself standing on a stage constructed in front of Holliday House, dressed in a tangerine-and-hot-pink Jalisco skirt and matching ruffled blouse as she waited for a Baile Folklórico performance to begin.

A half dozen other women similarly garbed

and an equal number of men in charro suits stood around her, warming up with rapid ball-ball-heel-heel movements and swaying their arms to loosen their joints. Nikki had joined Baile Folklórico five years ago, helping to fill in their ranks when three members and their families were picked up and detained by ICE. She found that one way to deal with her impotence over the forced removal of her hard-working neighbors was to be their placeholder with Willamette Baile Folklórico.

"Good crowd today," she commented to Nadelyn Medina, a lawyer specializing in immigration rights, who, like Nikki, was fairly new to this style of dancing.

"I think my sweat is the size of marbles," Nadelyn said, plucking at her blouse. "Honestly, this is more nerve wracking than litigation."

Nikki laughed. "It's going to be great. They loved us last year."

"Seems like there are more people this year," Nadelyn worried, biting her thumbnail. "Does it seem to you that there are more people?"

Looking out on to the hustle and bustle of Holliday during a holiday, Nikki said, "I'm sure it's no more than average," though privately she agreed that the crowd appeared larger, and she, too, felt more nerves than usual, although she didn't think it was due to a larger-than-usual audience.

The first year she'd performed with the troupe, her whole family had come down to watch. Last year, Evan had cheered her on as her brother-in-law to be. He'd seemed genuinely impressed. Noah, then age five, had loved the swirl of her skirts and had her swish them around him like a matador while he pretended to be the bull.

Would Evan and Noah come today? The thought shot her nerves to additional heights. It was impossible to characterize her relationship with Evan right now. Friends turned lovers turned just friends turned in-laws-to-be turned just friends again turned friends pretending to be lovers?

And to think she had a degree in counseling.

Mariachis Del Valle had been strolling along Liberty Street, stopping from time to time to serenade the crowd. Now they gathered on the stage and began the opening bars of "El Son de la Negra," a folk song adapted by a Jaliscian composer and a very popular Baile Folklórico tune. As if her feet knew what to do without her, Nikki flowed onto the stage with the other dancers, stepping in time to the beat of her heart. Setting aside her personal concerns, she tapped, dipped her shoulders and swirled through the intricate steps, engaging the crowd, glancing out and smiling on turns toward the audience. And then she saw them.

With Noah perched atop his shoulders, Evan stood at the side of the stage where he wouldn't block anyone's view. He was always courteous like that.

Every time Nikki turned in their direction, her

eyes locked with his. Before she knew it, she was tapping more briskly, swaying more deeply and leaning into the exaggerated flirtation of the traditional dance.

There were five women dancing with five men, but each time Nikki twirled toward Evan, she saw that his eyes were on her and her alone. She was supposed to be flirting with her more experienced dance partner. Twice he cautioned through his wide performance smile, "Stick to the pattern!" But Evan's eyes burned, and concentration came at a premium. For a moment a thought emerged: What if she and Evan really were lovers, and Noah was her son?

"El Son de la Negra" ended with the men using wide-brimmed hats to cover their faces and the faces of their partners as they—supposedly— kissed. Nikki lost sight of Evan temporarily but made sure to look for him again before she took her place for the next dance.

At first, she thought he'd left the area, but then she spotted him still carrying Noah on his shoulders and now speaking to another person, too. Dressed in skinny jeans and an off-the-shoulder T-shirt in bright red, Anya grinned up at Noah, touching the child-sized running shoe that rested against Evan's chest.

A sense of primal possession made Nikki feel like a lioness. If Matteo, her dance partner, hadn't ushered her to the wings, where they had to re-enter for their next performance, she might have jumped off the stage and waded through the crowd to confront the other woman.

Confront her about what?

She'd never once felt jealous when another woman talked to Drew.

"What is the matter with you today?" Matteo frowned at her.

"What do you mean?"

"You forgot the steps. Frequently."

"I did? Sorry. I'll focus on the footwork next time."

As the next song began and the dancers moved out, Nikki made it as far as stage right before she began scanning the crowd.

Her feet slowed and her mood plummeted when she realized Evan had left the performance area. Last year he had stayed for the whole thing.

It never bothered you when Drew didn't come to the performance.

Matteo squeezed her hand as she missed another series of rapid steps. *"Aficionada,"* he grumbled. *Amateur.*

Why didn't it bother her that Drew hadn't been more involved in her life? She should have missed him when he wasn't here. They should have had a conversation about it. Or even an argument.

But last year when she had taken the stage on

Cinco de Mayo, knowing her fiancé was in Portland making a workout video he could have shot on his phone any day of the week, she hadn't missed him. Had not resented his absence from her life here in Holliday. She'd had Evan's eyes on her and Evan's smile and Noah's happy laughter to fill her up.

Why was I with Drew in the first place?

The question reverberated through her brain as she faced the audience for the portion of the dance where the women moved forward to entertain the crowd with *faldeos*, the sweeping arm rotations that made their skirts look like enormous butterfly wings.

Eden stood toward the front of the gathered crowd, holding a paper boat filled with food, from which she ate enthusiastically as she watched the show. She'd never missed one of Nikki's performances, nor was she inclined to say no to Felipa's delicious eats. As she focused on Nikki now, however, it was clear from her expression that she was concerned. "What's wrong?" she mouthed to her friend.

Uh oh. That meant Nikki had lost her smile. Plastering it on to her face again, she counseled herself to pay attention to what she was doing for the rest of the performance. The moment they were done, she made a beeline for Eden. Evan and Noah, she noted, were nowhere in sight.

"What's going on?" her best friend asked between bites of yucca fries.

"Where's Gideon?" Nikki asked. It was almost six in the evening. Unless they were working, Eden and her fiancé were almost always together nowadays.

"He's speaking at a grief support group tonight."

"You miss him, right?"

Eden looked at her curiously. "He's just in Portland."

"But you wish he was with you."

"Well, of course. He's never experienced a Cinco de Mayo, Holliday-style. He's going to plan for it next year. I was going to save him some yucca fries, but they're much better fresh than reheated. I'll just go ahead and finish them."

"A-ha! So you do miss him."

Eden bit the tip off another fry, chewed and swallowed. "Maybe lay off the energy drinks some, okay, hon? What is going on with you today?"

Nikki expelled a long breath. She felt exhausted. "I don't know. I guess being with Drew... It felt safe. It was easy. I mean, except for the organ meat issue."

Nodding, Eden handed her a yucca fry, which Nikki accepted readily. "But even then, I met all my goals. I'm fit, I have a career I love that lets me work school hours and school days so I can raise a family and I was about to get married to a man who said he wanted kids soon. I thought I had what

I wanted. But now… I feel like I should never have gotten engaged to him in the first place."

Eden nodded, her expression conveying love and sympathy, but not an iota of surprise.

Before Nikki could remark on that or question it, the Mariachis began to serenade the crowd with a traditional love song, inviting their audience to turn the area into a spontaneous dance floor. Eden and Nikki moved slightly off to the side as people accepted the invitation.

Among the dancers were Barney and Charlene Gleason, Eden's dear friends. Nikki, too, enjoyed spending time with the elderly couple, who hosted weekly Shabbat get-togethers in their home. Nikki had attended many of the Friday-night gatherings through the years, enjoying the company, the candle lighting and the heartfelt prayers of thanks and petition they were invited to share if they wanted to. More than once, Nikki had found herself privately praying for a relationship like Barney and Charlene's. Now, as she watched Barney accompany his bride of over forty years to the makeshift dance area, Nikki became awed again by their faith in each other.

Charlene had suffered a stroke the previous year and had spent quite a while in a wheelchair. Today, her mobility was supported only by a walker and her husband.

Setting the walker by their side, Barney took

his wife in his arms, supporting her slender body as she smiled into his crinkled eyes and leaned on him, swaying. It wasn't exactly "dancing" nor were they moving precisely to the beat of the music, but it was plain to see how in tune they were with each other. With life. With whatever movement in the universe turned people into best friends, life partners, lovers in the truest sense of the word. Barney and Charlene had "it." They had found meant-to-be and cherished it.

"You weren't surprised when I said I should never have gotten engaged to Drew," Nikki commented to Eden, her gaze still on the couple.

"I was surprised you said it," Eden corrected honestly. "But I don't disagree."

Nikki looked at her friend, torn between resentment and relief. "You never liked him, did you?"

"He's fine. Beyond all the external things you mentioned, I've never understood what he brought to the table for you. You and Evan always seemed to make much more sense. And now you're dating! Two years after you slept together. You crazy kids."

"Eden, you know we're not *actually* dating—"

Eden gave her a look that said she didn't really believe Nikki and Evan were still just friends.

Guilty for not trying harder to convince her friend of the truth, Nikki felt her mood plummet further. Eden read her expression as a different kind of concern. "Hey, even confirmed bachelors can change their minds. Look at Gideon. And George Clooney."

Anxiety sat heavily in the center of Nikki's chest. "Yeah."

"Yeah...but what?"

"I don't want to find out two years from now when I'm almost forty that Evan is a confirmed bachelor after all." Tears stung her eyes as the truth of her words hit home. "I already...care about him, and..." She shook her head.

Eden squeezed Nikki's arm. "I know. It feels like way too big a risk. But refusing to fall in love may be an even bigger risk than going ahead and doing it. There's a consequence either way. You're already such good friends and you're 'pretending' you're in a relationship. Can you stay in the moment a while longer and see what happens? Figure out how you really feel about each other?"

Eden's words played on a loop in Nikki's head. She wasn't sure what to say. So instead, she commented, "Charlene seems to be doing well."

Accepting the abrupt change in topic, Eden agreed. "She is!" Eden, who viewed the Gleasons almost as a second set of parents, launched into a narration of all the physical improvements Charlene had made since her stroke. As someone who'd done more than her fair share of physical therapy and was now engaged to a doctor, Eden sounded as if she knew what she was talking about. "So where's

Evan?" Eden asked once she'd exhausted the previous topic. "I thought I saw him."

"Oh yeah, you probably did. He's…around. With Noah." *And Anya.*

The jealousy that erupted from that thought made Nikki's face feel hotter than the dancing had.

"Are you blushing?" Eden stared at her. "Or are you upset? I can't tell."

"Blushing." Nikki chose the answer that required the lesser amount of explanation. "Definitely blushing."

"Awww." Eden nudged Nikki with her shoulder. "Ya know…someday, you and Evan could be like Barney and Charlene." She nodded toward the couple, who had dreamy smiles on their faces as they swayed to the music. "Stranger things have happened."

The suggestion set off a reaction that felt like an impending panic attack. No doubt about it, she was going over the edge. Nothing in her body or mind seemed to make any sense anymore. She hadn't been this confused about relationships since she was a teenager.

"You're blushing again!" Eden marveled.

"Yeah, well." Where was an air conditioner—or a Xanax drip—when you needed it? "Let's not jump the gun about anything."

Eden smiled knowingly. "That's what I kept thinking about Gideon and look where we are now."

Eating the last fry, she wagged her head smugly. "If you ask me, love is in the air in Holliday. Why fight it?"

Evan handled Mother's Day the way he'd handle a toothache: suffer through until the pain receded.

In Holliday, Oregon, Mother's Day was, of course, a very big deal. Members of the Mother's Day Committee (this town had a committee for everything) stationed themselves along Liberty Street to hand out red roses to every woman who walked past, parent status notwithstanding. The Holliday Fruit & Nut Co. packaged individual bags of chocolate-covered marionberries and offered them to anyone who identified as a mother, aunt, grandmother, childcare worker… Hell, if you'd ever smiled at a toddler in this town you could swing by for a sugar fix.

Every women's apparel store in Holliday offered a discount, restaurants opened early for brunch, and, if you didn't have family nearby to treat you, the Mothers & Others Brunch in the community center had you covered.

All that, however, was on Sunday, two days away. Evan thought he might take Noah to the zoo, distract him from the roses and chocolates and moms. Today, Friday, they just had to get through "Special Person's Day" at Noah's school. Then they'd be home free.

Jogging up the concrete steps to the elementary building, Evan forced an enthusiasm he didn't feel. The stately eighty-year-old brick building had been renovated a couple years ago and now had rather elegant tempered-glass doors that led to a sleek entryway, courtesy of the Holliday Family Foundation. A large A-frame sign out front announced, Special Person's Day in Your Child's Classroom.

Walking through the building to the first-grade wing, Evan realized the near-empty hallways meant he was late. His eighth graders were reading Sherman Alexie's *The Absolutely True Diary of a Part-Time Indian*, and he'd wanted to make sure they had substantive discussion questions before he turned his classroom over to the ministrations of the sub he'd asked to cover for him this afternoon.

Laughter, chatter and the aroma of popcorn drifted through open classroom doors. By the time he reached the first-grade pod, Evan was both hungry and nervous about Noah most likely being the only kid without a mother or grandmother present. The administration could reclassify the day however they wanted, but everyone knew—the kids, in particular, knew—that this was a celebration intended to honor moms.

As the familiar sense of failure and guilt rose to engulf him, Evan reminded himself that he was being mindful and purposeful about his life. Sometimes, though, he worried that he was doing what his father had done: giving his son a life without a healthy female influence. He hated that but refused to repeat the pattern of introducing a series of women through Noah's life, allowing him to begin to love and trust someone only to replace that sweetness with the bitterness of confusion and grief when the relationship ended through no fault of his own. No. He'd rather be alone the rest of his life than put his son through that.

Like his father, Evan had chosen a partner who had as many problems as he in the area of personal relationships; that's why Noah was effectively a single-parent child. God willing Noah would break the cycle and have a partner relationship that was warm, loving and emotionally intimate. Living in Holliday and surrounding Noah with caring people may be as close as Evan could get to a picket-fence life, but Noah would be able to go further someday.

Pausing outside the door to Ms. Cheney's room, Evan tried consciously to let go of his negative thoughts before he entered, so he could give his best to his boy. Noah had asked Nikki to be his "special person" today, and she'd agreed, but she had a lot on her mind, and they hadn't connected since Cinco de Mayo. She'd gone home after her performance, unlike the previous year when they'd enjoyed the celebration far into the evening. He didn't know if she'd remember about today.

After agreeing to look at Anya's car to help her

figure out why the engine wouldn't turn over (it had started up fine for him, so he'd recommended getting the battery checked), he'd headed back to the stage area, where Nikki had been nowhere to be found. He'd texted to ask if she wanted to grab dinner, but she hadn't responded until the next day and even then she'd been brief. He didn't want the fake relationship to ruin the real thing and felt like kicking himself in the ass for pushing it. For Noah's sake, he'd fix things, though he wasn't quite certain how.

The first thing Evan saw when he rounded the door to the classroom was color. Noah's teacher filled her room with artwork, crafts and posters. Like last year, too-small chairs arranged around tables were filled with women of varying ages, likely mothers and grandmothers. Evan would have appreciated a two-dad family or even another single father like him to alleviate the sore-thumb phenomenon. The kids ate bright orange cheese puffs stuffed into paper cups and tiny cookies the size of quarters that sat on napkins in front of them while the women admired artwork created in their honor. *Damn, I'm really late.* From just inside the doorway, Evan scanned the room, searching for Noah's table, which changed monthly. He'd been seated near the walkingsticks aquarium last month but must have moved. Ms. Cheney was across the room, preparing a craft project. Other than calling out his son's name, Evan was limited to a visual search as his blood pressure spiked. He recalled exactly what it felt like to have someone else's mother take pity on him when one of his stepmothers hadn't shown at some function.

There he is. Immediately upon spotting Noah, Evan took a step forward. In the process of squeezing between two small tables, nodding at the mothers who glanced up at him, he stopped abruptly. Noah wasn't with someone who'd taken pity on him.

In an ankle-length pastel-colored dress dotted with tiny flowers, a cropped sweater and a flower-covered headband, Nikki sat beside Noah, pointing to the card he'd made for her and telling him what she loved about it.

"Did you really draw this amazing cat all by yourself? Really-truly-cross-your-heart-agree-to-lick-a-frog-if-you're-fibbing honest?" When Noah nodded vigorously, Nikki hugged him to her then pointed to one of the small cups of fluorescent snack food. "Are these my cheese puffs?"

Slipping back to the door, Evan watched his son and best friend as they chatted and laughed, and Nikki taught Noah to squash the cheese puffs like an accordion between his thumb and forefinger before eating them, sprinkling neon cheese dust everywhere. Ms. Cheney was going to love *that*.

Face alive with joy, Noah drummed his feet on the floor and bounced on his seat, pointing out the friendship flags hanging from a string that stretched from wall to wall.

Pivoting to the hallway, Evan paused a few steps away from the classroom and took several deep breaths. Relief and gratitude felt good, but fear rushed at him, too. The gratitude toward Nikki, the appreciation for her friendship and the love she'd showered on them both, felt tsunami-like in its strength. The intensity of feeling was both a gift and a big problem. A gift because Noah reaped the benefits of Nikki's loyalty. A problem because Evan could no longer deny that he felt less "friendly" toward Nikki and more…something else.

After realizing he'd started to perspire, he swiped a hand across his forehead. He should go back to work but felt faintly nauseous, strangely shaky, and the sub was already there. Maybe he just needed food.

Evan started down the hallway, body and head seeming disconnected. His feet carried him out of the school building, but his mind remained in the classroom, watching Nikki, the closest thing to a mother his son had known.

The only woman he couldn't imagine ever losing.

Chapter Eleven

Weddings brought out the best and the worst in the guests. The best were the dreamy smiles and wistful tears of people who remembered their own weddings with gratitude and love. The best also emerged in the laughter and celebrating of young people recently married themselves or still looking forward to that joyous occasion.

The worst could usually be seen in the public restrooms of whatever venue hosted the reception, where former partners of the marrying couple tended to break down in unhappy tears or talk of ripping their former partner a new one, proving that open bars were not the best idea when emotions ran high anyway.

The wedding of Ryan Berman and Ollison Mackin IV promised lots of drama, but not necessarily the negative kind. They'd been together for years. All former partners had long since had their say and moved on. The drama tonight came from Ollison's creative background (artistic director of a live theatre venue in Portland), the entertainment he'd chosen for the reception, the design and the mysterious material-covered easel that sat at the front of the ballroom, waiting to be unveiled.

"Are all these lights stage lights?" Evan leaned into Nikki's space at their round table, asking the question in his smooth baritone, his aftershave wafting over her with notes of citrus and the sea.

"Yes. Ollison had them brought in for the performances that will happen later," she confirmed.

"Performances?"

After a touching ceremony, the newly married couple was seated at a head table, holding hands. Ryan's wheelchair was tucked closely to his husband's chair in the ballroom that Ollison had designed to resemble a large dinner theatre.

Ryan had been a high-school senior when the SUV in which he, Eden and their mother were driving rolled over, permanently injuring him and leaving Eden with scars inside and out.

A steadfast love had been hard to come by for both Berman siblings, but Eden had found her forever with their sometimes-taciturn town doctor, and

Ryan… Well, Ryan had had the good sense to fall in love with a man who possessed a heart of gold, impeccable taste and a flair for entertainment. With a degree in scenic design, and theatre in his blood, Ollison had overseen every aspect of their Broadway-themed wedding, and he'd shared his ideas liberally with Nikki, whose own wedding had been planned at the Oregon Garden in Silverton. It promised to be less theatrical but just as visually appealing.

"Ollison recruited actors from his company and from a musical theatre company called Broadway Rose to perform numbers from Tony-winning musicals," she whispered to Evan since it was supposed to be a surprise for the guests. Every time she leaned in to him—during the ceremony and now—she believed the hype about pheromones. Aftershave aside, she'd always loved the way he smelled—like comfort and steadiness and home, all the intangible goodness that made him such a valued friend…

All the intangible goodness that, lately, made her want to jump his damn bones.

Pulling back, Nikki sat up straight and proper on her red slipcovered seat. All evening long, Evan had been his charming, platonically attentive, very appropriate self, damn it. After much thought and a fair amount of prayer, several pros-and-cons lists and two online compatibility quizzes (she'd answered on his behalf), Nikki was sure…pretty sure…they should take their relationship to the next-level. She wasn't being wishy-washy; she *did* want to move out of the friend zone, but there was a lot to lose here if it didn't work out. There was a friendship she treasured. And there was Noah.

She loved that kid. Being his "Special Person" at school, making him feel special in turn, had filled her up far more than seeing herself on Drew's Instagram #bodygoals ever could. Noah had been proud to have her there, sitting with all the moms, not because of anything she'd done, but because he felt her love. That was it. That, she'd discovered, was everything.

"This is deep-fried asparagus with a truffle aioli," announced a handsome young server who placed a basket in front of them and two more for the other couples at their table.

Evan peered hungrily at the basket, then arched a brow playfully. "Noah says ''Sparagus is smelly,' and I tend to agree, but I'll try one if you will."

"I love asparagus."

He cocked his head. "How did I not know this about you?"

A sexy, mischievous glint lit Evan's eyes. It was an expression she'd seen dozens of times. It didn't mean anything. Until today. Today, that look filled her with *lust*. The whole room fell away. They were all alone, and she was starving, but not for asparagus.

What if they had sex again? It had been two years.

He looked so beautiful in his dove-gray suit.

Golden-brown hair and eyes the color of the sky at Seaside made her want to lean in for a kiss *sooooo bad*...

Would making love change his mind (this time) about relationships? Would he want something—something long-term—with *her*?

Would he dive into love...

...turn "long-term" into "forever"...

Anxiety shot through Nikki's veins like a bullet train. *Forever...forever...forever...*

She'd wanted that with Drew, had expected it and had felt comforted by the thought. Why did "forever" with Evan seem at once more wonderful and *so much more* terrifying?

"Do you?"

She realized he'd been talking to her. Her mouth felt so dry. She swallowed. "Do I what?"

"Want some?"

Oh, hell yes. Then she realized he was holding a fried asparagus spear.

Hardly able to sit still, she felt constricted, as if her dress were glued to her body. Speaking of the dress...

She'd bought it just for him. Bold fuchsia, bias hem just over her knees in the front, off the shoulder and a bodice that hugged her the way she wished he would.

If they made love again, maybe they wouldn't

have forever. Maybe that was too much to expect. Maybe she needed to release expectations.

Maybe she should stop thinking.

Evan intended for her to take the asparagus with her fingers; that was clear. Instead, she leaned forward, her eyes never leaving his, as she parted her fuchsia-painted lips and took a bite, straightening up and chewing without once breaking their gaze.

The look in Evan's eyes morphed from comedy to drama in a heartbeat. Couldn't take that action back, and she didn't want to. Maybe it was time to be a little reckless. The idea terrified her.

Lips pressed together, Evan breathed more heavily. His gently flaring nostrils and lowered brow combined to make him appear a tad dangerous. Which he was, to her.

"Nikki." He said only her name, hoarsely spoken. She'd never felt such anticipation in her life.

"Friends and family, the grooms have a surprise they would like to share with you now!" The DJ interrupted whatever else Evan had been about to say.

Evan swallowed, seeming as if he might speak again, but a booming musical fanfare prevented conversation. With his eyes still on her, he pulled back. As Ollison and Ryan made their way to the stage, Ryan guiding his wheelchair up the ramp built for that purpose, Evan turned his attention to the dais, though his profile remained tense.

Dang it!

Nikki had been anticipating Ry and Olli's wedding for months. Now she had to breathe deeply in order to remain in her chair and focus on these two precious people instead of on Evan. (And on her body's response to Evan, which *gurrrrl…*) Ryan and Olli had found and committed to each other despite life's complications, perhaps because of life's complications. They'd been each other's safe harbor for a long time.

Together, they positioned themselves beside the covered easel.

"At this time, Ryan and Ollison would like their families to join them on the stage."

Eden, who'd served as Ryan's "Best Sister" at the ceremony, walked to the stage with Gideon, followed by her and Ryan's parents. Nikki was happy to see Mrs. Berman looking better than she had in ages. After a long bout with addiction to prescription meds, Eden's mother seemed to be following her children's lead in letting go of the past and choosing to move forward.

Ollison's mother, his sister, the sister's husband and their teenage daughter and son joined the group around the easel. In their formal clothes, they made a beautiful picture. The photographer snapped photos as people raised their phones to capture the moment for themselves.

"There's someone missing from the family portrait," announced the DJ. Anticipation built as Ollison placed one hand on the material covering the easel. A drumroll sounded. "Introducing for the very first time, Matthew Mackin-Berman!"

Over Boyce Avenue's cover of "With Arms Wide Open," gasps and cheers erupted in a thunderous ovation. Balloons and confetti rained down as Ryan and Ollison beamed over a poster-sized portrait of a little boy around five years old. Family hugged, friends shouted their congratulations, video rolled.

"Did you know about this?" Evan asked as they stood to applaud along with the rest of the guests.

"I knew they were adopting, but I didn't realize they'd been matched."

Eden seemed as surprised as anyone. Tears streamed down her face as she hugged her brother, then Olli, then her parents before clasping one of Gideon's hands in hers. Her free hand moved to her own belly and rested there.

"I knew it," Nikki whispered, filled with unbridled joy *and* the deepest grief she'd ever experienced. Her best friend was pregnant, no doubt about it. After the auto accident that had left her scarred, Eden had not been certain she could have children. For a number of years, she'd refused to try. Then she'd met Gideon and discovered that when your soul felt safe you were willing to take risks that were too frightening otherwise. Nikki's eyes filled with tears of gratitude over the blessing her friend of nearly twenty years had received.

A napkin appeared in front of her. Evan watched her, equal parts wary and sympathetic.

About to turn the napkin down as unnecessary, Nikki realized her cheeks were wet and her eyes blurry. "Thank you."

Quite likely, her eye makeup was running, but the tears kept coming. When she spoke to Eden, she wanted to add to the collective happiness, not be a cause for concern.

"Back in a sec," she murmured wetly to Evan, taking the napkin with her as she went to the nearest women's restroom. It appeared she was going to be the person who inevitably wound up in the bathroom crying at someone else's wedding. *Blech.* She had to pull herself together. Unfortunately, as she entered the restroom, the tears continued and she realized these were tears of grief for herself. Thirty-seven wasn't *old.* Women had babies in their fifties. (Not easily.) The thing was, she'd always imagined a large, boisterous family with babies and grand-babies and a husband who were all…well…*hers.*

Relieved that the lounge was empty, she went immediately to the tissue box, pulled out several and started wiping the mascara and eyeliner that were, indeed, smeared raccoon-like beneath her eyes. Every time she wiped it away, more tears and a seemingly endless supply of black makeup flowed to take its place.

She adored her parents and esteemed adoption;

as a teen she'd penned a very positive article for *Adoption Today* magazine. That didn't take away the feeling that there was something missing—a hole in her soul she'd never been able to fill. Getting engaged to Drew had seemed to occupy that space. Having babies certainly would have. Without the family she'd dreamed of, maybe that missing piece would remain missing.

More tears, more tissues and a reapplication of mascara got her ready to return to the reception.

As she left the women's room, she very deliberately put a smile on her face, preparing to share her friends' joy. It slipped off the moment she saw who was waiting for her.

After pushing away from a giant pillar, Evan stood still, watching her. How long had he been there? She didn't ask, and he didn't say. He didn't ask why she'd left so abruptly, either, or how she was now, though the question was in his eyes.

The air here in the hotel lobby was cool, the surroundings opulent with golden tones, polished floors and crystal fixtures. She and Evan were dressed to the nines. The stiletto sandals that added four inches to her petite stature had made her feel sexy as all get out when she'd put them on tonight, but even with the added height, Evan still had eight or ten inches on her. His beautiful broad shoulders, wide chest and strong arms made her breath quicken. And his eyes…

His eyes were not deliberately seductive. On the contrary: They were sober, a bit sad and wholly intent on her.

He walked toward her slowly. When he reached his hand to her, she took it. Perhaps all he'd intended was to escort her back to the ballroom, yet once their fingertips touched they melded into each other and the kiss they shared seemed neither timid nor hungry; it happened as if they'd been kissing all their lives.

Nikki didn't know how long they stood there. When the kiss ended, they walked back to the reception looking at each other, their hands still clasped.

It seemed unbelievably natural to congratulate Ryan and Ollison, then Eden (who blushed profusely, but did not deny that she was pregnant!). It felt natural to dance with Evan then watch Olli's musical theatre friends perform Broadway tunes about love and friendship and forever, then dance some more and eat cake. Nikki and Evan had the same good time they'd have enjoyed before there'd been any tension between them, but this time a current of electric awareness buzzed through every move.

Ryan had chosen *Something Good* from *The Sound of Music* as the song he wanted to dedicate to Ollison. When the DJ invited everyone onto the dance floor, Evan pulled Nikki toward him for the slow dance and said, "I played Captain Von Trapp in high school."

"You did not. You sing?"

"Badly. But I was the only drama student taller than the leading lady."

He proceeded to croon the song softly in her ear as they slow danced, and there was nothing bad about it—not his voice or the stirring of his warm breath against her ear or the feel of his strong, solid body pressed to hers.

Something had changed, and it wasn't ever going to change back. For Nikki, there was an excitement and a danger in the knowledge. Two years ago, they'd been able to return to friendship. That wouldn't be an option this time, not for her. She'd passed the point of no return.

The party continued well past midnight, not necessarily too late to head back to Holliday if they'd wanted to, but Noah didn't have to be picked up until the following afternoon. As the reception wound to a close with embraces and final congratulations, Eden and Gideon mentioned they were staying at the hotel, as were Ryan and Olli. That might have been an influence, or Nikki and Evan might have made their decision already. Impulses seemed less clear after midnight.

In any case, the outcome remained the same. Hand in hand, they walked to the hotel lobby, booked a room and stared at each other in the elevator, the tension and heat between them turning the damn thing into a sauna. Nikki couldn't trust herself to kiss Evan yet; she knew she wouldn't stop. They'd waited far, far too long to make love again for her not to lose control once she went all in. And, she was all in. Without any clue where this was going to lead, she was ready to follow her heart…at least into the hotel room.

His eyes smoldering like the bluest part of a flame, Evan continued to stare at her as he swiped the room card across the keypad. Their hands were still clasped while he opened the door, pocketed the card and waited less than a second to bend his head to hers. Devoid of the pretense of restraint, he kissed her, letting go of her hand and reaching around to lift her into his arms.

The kiss felt…*right*. Unbelievably right. With her hand, Nikki pushed open the door so they could enter the room. Using his foot, Evan kicked it shut again to give them all the privacy they needed as they began to correct the wrong from two years past.

The problem wasn't that they'd made love when they shouldn't have. The problem was that they'd stopped.

Nikki had insisted on driving her car from Holliday to Ryan and Olli's wedding in Portland, because Evan was doing her the favor of being her plus one.

It seemed only right to do the driving. Now she was glad she had control of the wheels as she pulled up outside her parents' home at six the morning after the ceremony. She'd slept…not at all. Still, she was as wired as if she'd chased a triple shot with an energy drink.

Evan had slept soundly while she'd fished around for her clothes and gotten dressed. She'd written a quick note, saying she'd be back before checkout, though she hoped to return before he even opened his eyes.

Ordinarily after making love as they had last night, she'd be asleep half the day.

That was a lie. She'd never made love the way they had last night.

Making love with Evan involved passion like she'd never known—ever. The first time they'd slept together, she'd held part of herself back; she could see that now. She'd protected her heart, because falling in love with him was so, so, so much more terrifying than falling in love with anyone else, including his brother.

It wasn't as if she'd been insincere when she'd gotten engaged to Drew. Commitment, expectation and hope had been on the table. She'd felt happy and relaxed planning their wedding and future family. Why, then, had she spent the wee hours of this morning lying next to Evan in a cold, misery-inducing anxious sweat, trying with all her weak-

ened might not to leave him a note saying this had
been a mistake—again?

She'd texted her mother at five o'clock, looking
for an answer. Rivka was a devotee of mindfulness
meditation and arose at four every morning to begin
her practice. Rivka also had her phone charged and
by her side 24/7 lest one of her children, their partners, a grandchild or distant relative needed her.

I'm in town. Coffee and bagels? I'll stop on the
way, Nikki had texted, receiving an immediate response: Can't get a decent bagel in PDX before 7,
but I'm here for you, baby. I'll send Dad to the golf
course. Come at six. Don't bring anything.

Rivka's text proved two things: 1.) Her mother
had a sixth sense and knew exactly when her children needed her and only her, and 2.) The woman
was still ordering her bagels (and quite likely
smoked cod) from New York despite delis and bagel
shops popping up all over Portland.

Walking up to the house in heels and a formal
gown felt weird in the extreme, but she'd be able to
brush her teeth and change clothes here. Her mother
insisted on keeping the guest room stocked with
clothes and toiletries for each of her children "in
case of emergencies."

Rivka opened the door seconds before Nikki rang
the bell, looked her daughter up and down, tamed
the concern in her eyes with a beneficent smile,
warm hug, and instructed, "Come in, bubaleh. Cof-

fee and conversation in the kitchen. First, go upstairs to change clothes." With a hand rubbing her
daughter's back, she urged Nikki to the staircase.
"I got you a darling new jogging suit from Wind-
sor in the mall. Normally not my type of place—so
many booby tops." (Her mother's term for anything
revealing.) "Cousin Marion's granddaughter Isabel
got her first job there, so I made an exception. This
time. Did you have a toothbrush with you last night?
I'm guessing not. There are several new ones in the
guest bathroom. Take your pick. Up you go." She
pushed Nikki gently up the first step. "Then come
to the kitchen, and I'll explain everything."

What was sometimes maddening—her mother's
chatter, the direction, the apparent non sequiturs—
felt, today, like a balm for Nikki's fired-up nerves.
She walked up two carpeted steps then turned.
"Wait. *You'll* explain everything?"

Rivka inhaled deeply, let the breath go and nodded. "I think it's time we had 'the talk.'"

Across the kitchen table, Rivka had spread the
contents of a box she kept on her office bookshelf.
Labeled Nikki's Adoption, it contained a Guatemalan birth certificate, her parents' home study in
English and Spanish, a report detailing her birth
mother's history and reason for making an adoption plan, DNA evidence proving they were indeed
birth mother and birth daughter and photos mark-

ing Nikki's time in Guatemala as an infant. Nikki had seen it all before. She'd chosen to leave the information in its box on the bookshelf because…she didn't know why.

This morning, over Brooklyn Bagels (only boiled-then-baked were worth the calories according to her mother) and a strong cup of Guatemalan Antigua coffee, Rivka described—not for the first time—the process of adopting Nikki.

"They said we should get a lot of sleep, because when we took you from your foster mother you'd cry for the first twenty-four hours. You didn't, though. You reached your arms out for me and I took you, and it was magic. My *life* was magic from that moment on."

Rivka casually looked at the pages she'd laid out. "You were my *bashert*, my meant-to-be. Born in my soul. The way we met here on earth was never a concern. That was God's business."

The story was the same one Nikki had been told since the time before memory. She wondered why Rivka was telling it again today, but it was soothing nonetheless. Nikki's desire to unload her worry and questions and fears about her relationship with Evan seemed to take its place on a conversational back burner, simmering but not needing to be stirred just yet.

"What are you telling me, Mom?"

Rivka looked up. "Finding love can be as terrifying as losing love."

"Right. Unfortunately, that's not really clarifying anything for me."

Pushing her glasses to the top of her head so that they nestled in the soft strawberry blond waves, Rivka smiled from the deep well of her love for her daughter. Nikki had always found her mother's hair so lovely. The day she'd realized she and her mom had completely different coloring—when she was five years old and her best friend, Frances, pointed out in a worried tone that Nikki and her mother's skin color "don't match"—Nikki had decided that soft strawberry blonde waves, blue eyes and ivory skin were the best combination to have. For some reason, that memory pinched her heart today.

Seated on the banquette beneath the corner window in the Chois' sunny kitchen, Rivka reached across the table to take one of Nikki's hands gently in both of hers. "I love all my children. My heart is like a house where you each have a room forever. But you, my first… With you, I always worry that you think the room isn't big enough, or that it's not decorated right."

"What? Mom, what are you talking about? Wait…it's almost my birthday. Is this about the 'primal wound'? I'm adopted, so I have a hole you'll never be able to fill? Because if that *is* what this is about, we've talked it through before, and I promise I'm okay. You and Dad and Gia and sometimes Lev when he's not being bombastic—kidding, I love Levvie—you're my family through and through. Yes, I went through a rough patch as a teen, but there is absolutely nothing you didn't give me. Nothing you need to 'fix' now or compensate for, and please tell that to Gia, because sometimes she drives me crazy with her bio-born guilt." Nikki smiled, squeezing her mother's hands.

Rivka patted Nikki, sat back against the brightly flowered banquette cushions and said, "Good. I'll get right to the point, then. Two years ago, you were in love with Evan. You're still in love with Evan. Close your mouth. I'm your mother, and I'm a lot older than you so I see what I see. Why are children always surprised about that?" She shook her head. "Last time you weren't willing to fight for it—and I'm not talking about fighting with him or against him. He's got his own *mishigas* to contend with. We're all a little bit burdened. I'm talking about you fighting your own fear. It's easier to settle for mediocre than to fight for what you really want and maybe not get it."

Awkward. "Is this what happens when you become a mother?" Nikki muttered. "You develop the superpower of X-ray vision and make your children feel naked?"

"Yes!" Rivka slapped the edge of the table and smiled. "That's exactly what happens. A little gift

from heaven to make up for all the sleepless nights."
Picking up her coffee cup, she then took a sip. "My
point is you're in love with Evan. This time, you
should be a Nachshon."

"A Nachshon." Following this conversation was
going to give Nikki a headache for the rest of the
day. Her tired brain searched through its files.
"Nachshon. Are you talking about the guy who
jumped into the Red Sea?"

"Exactly. When the waters are raging and no one
can imagine a way through, someone has to take
the first step." Making a fist, Rivka placed it on her
stomach. "And that person is the one who knows in
her *kishkes* what she should do and won't let fear get
in the way." Satisfied that her daughter understood
her point, Rivka sat back, nursing her coffee cup.

Nikki shook her head. "I think you're telling me
to take a chance with Evan, right? But it's not that
simple. First of all, I'm not saying I'm *in love* with
Evan Northrup. We could maybe explore the possibility of a relationship."

"Maybe explore the possibility? Were you with
Evan at this wedding last night?" her mother asked.

"Yes, I was."

"And you stayed *together* in the hotel? Where he
didn't have his pajamas, either?"

"Mom! That's—"

Rivka waved both her hands. "Fine, fine, I don't
need to know." She leaned forward, blue eyes more

piercing than gently maternal. "Listen, my girl, love *is* the Red Sea. All love. Becoming a parent, being someone's child, falling in love romantically—the water starts rising around you and you begin to think, *Oy vey, what if I get in over my head?* And you know what? You *will* get in over your head, guaranteed. If not immediately, someday for certain. So what do you do about it? Jump in."

It felt to Nikki that the Red Sea was raging inside her at that very moment.

Just *jump in*?

She looked out the window, watching the morning sky turn to pastel blue. "It really…isn't that simple, Mom."

"Hmm." Doubt dripped from the word.

"Well, it isn't! Evan's not someone who wants commitment."

"What's your evidence?"

"He hasn't dated anyone seriously in six years. Maybe he's still in love with Noah's mother. I have no idea, because he won't talk about it except to say he thinks marriage was one of the great gifts in life."

"That's not entirely logical. Either Evan doesn't like commitment, or he's *so* committed that he's emotionally tied to a woman six years after seeing her for the last time. Pick one."

Nikki pulled off a piece of bagel, dragged it

through cream cheese and chewed. "You're confusing me. I think I need to journal about this."

Rivka smiled. "Overthinking this is the last thing you need to do."

"You're my mother. Aren't you concerned that I could get serious about someone who may still be committed to someone else in his heart?"

"No, I'm not concerned." She shrugged. "I asked him about it a long time ago." Rivka passed Nikki a napkin. "Here, spit the bagel out. You sound like you're choking."

When her coughing jag ended, Nikki stared incredulously. "You asked about Mikaela?"

"Of course. You haven't?"

"He doesn't like to talk about it."

"So? We're as sick as our secrets. Evan is a lovely man. Why would I want him to be sick? I asked if he still loved Noah's mother; he answered."

Nikki waited for her mother to expound. When that didn't happen, Nikki prodded, "What did he say?"

Rivka shook her head regretfully. "I told him he could tell me in confidence—just like I do with you kids. The only thing I can tell you right now is I love you, I'm here for you, and I will always, always be. And, if you think losing Evan and that little boy of his could hurt you more than losing any other future you can imagine, then they're your Red Sea. And if they're your Red Sea, jump."

Chapter Twelve

Nikki got what she came for when she talked to her mother. The adoption materials had been a not-so-subtle reminder that life could be beautiful, surprising and completely beyond control. When that lesson came so early in life that you had no way to process it, fear came and stayed, altering the way you walked through life.

On the drive back to the downtown hotel, Nikki thought about her broken engagement and cried. The grief was beginning to hit her—not sadness for the loss of Drew or their future together, but grief because she'd spent two whole years of her life with a man she hadn't wildly loved and who clearly hadn't wildly loved her, either. Drew hadn't broken her heart by changing his mind; she'd never given him enough of her heart to make that possible.

It was eight thirty on a sun-filled Sunday morning in May when Nikki used the key card to let herself into the room she'd shared with Evan. She'd been anxious when she'd left earlier, but the memory of him carrying her into the room brought a return of the feelings of anticipation and passion. She hoped he was still in bed.

She didn't want to talk, didn't want to analyze, didn't want to discern his thoughts on where they stood in their relationship. All she wanted was another opportunity to feel the wild, completely out-of-control longing to spend her life wrapped in his arms.

A few steps into the room, she realized with a thud of disappointment that the drapes had been drawn. Visions of shucking her sweats and climbing back into bed with Evan faded away completely when she saw him standing at the window, his broad back and excellent shoulders bare, but the lower part of his body dressed in last night's trousers. Even from the back, she could tell his body was tight. A feeling of intense misgiving made her pause in the doorway.

She'd entered their room quietly so as not to awaken him until she climbed back into bed (where she'd planned to awaken him plenty). Even though he was already up, he was so deeply absorbed by his thoughts that he hadn't heard her.

Trepidation sounded like white water in her ears. She had a brief urge to slip out the way she'd come in but shook her head at it. *Jump in.*

"Morning." Using cheerfulness to cut a swath through the tension, Nikki walked toward him, stopping at the opposite side of the small dining table positioned by the window.

Evan turned, his brow taut and his jaw clenched, eyes impossible to read.

Refusing to let her heart sink, Nikki smiled. "I went to see my mom. Did you read my note? She sent bagels—" Nikki raised a plastic bag "—but I thought it might be more fun to order something in. Have breakfast in bed."

Evan's brow lifted, and he blinked several times—less to indicate he approved of her suggestion and more indicative that he was only just now processing that she was, in fact, back in the room. Nikki ignored her disappointment; she'd process that later. Trying to discern her next move, she decided, *What the hell…*

Raising a hand to her collarbone, she took hold of the zipper on the cropped sweat suit jacket and lowered it slowly, hearing the metallic buzz of the zipper and watching Evan's eyes widen.

He doesn't look disappointed.

She kept going, allowing the little jacket to

slip down her arms, off her hands and drop to the carpeted floor. "We don't have to check out until eleven. Unless there's something wrong?"

Standing in a fuchsia lace bra that barely covered anything, Nikki realized the *Is there anything wrong?* probably could have come a bit earlier, but…in for a penny, in for a pound.

When Evan shook his head slowly, she remained nonchalant. "Oh, good."

Reaching for the waistband of her sweatpants, she kept her eyes on Evan (including the chest and abs that were making it a bit harder to breathe) and wriggled until they, too, fell to the floor.

Evan's gaze lowered to her…panties. *Oops.*

"My mother keeps a change of clothes for me," she said of the decidedly unsexy panty selection. "She's more of a 100% cotton gal."

"They definitely don't match your bra." Evan sounded as if he could use a drink of water. "It's a little jarring." He walked around to her, standing so close that he didn't have to reach far at all to hook a finger inside the elastic band around her hips. "Mind if I take them off?"

Nikki felt a smile in her chest. "Not if you find them upsetting."

"Oh, I do. I definitely do."

The cotton underwear joined the sweatpants, and Evan pulled Nikki to him for a kiss that lifted her off the ground. Wrapping her legs around his waist and her arms tightly around his shoulders, she grinned against his lips as he walked her to the bed, where they finished removing every physical barrier between them.

"Aunt Nikki, can we play Qwirkle after this?"

"What? You're already talking about the next game?" Plucking a piece of popcorn from the bowl on the coffee table, where they'd set up their game, she tossed it over the top of Noah's game board. "We haven't finished Battleship yet."

"J-16!" he called.

As he approached seven years old, he was picking up the game's strategy with remarkable speed. Plus, Nikki clustered all her ships in one place, making the game easier for him. Now she slapped her jeans-covered thigh. "Aw, you sunk my battleship."

Noah thrust both his arms in the air. "I win! Dad," he said excitedly as Evan entered from the kitchen, "wanna play Qwirkle?"

Evan set a plate of broadly sliced carrots and a bowl of his homemade spicy peanut sauce on the table beside the popcorn. "It's time to start thinking about dinner." He sat on the couch, close to Nikki.

In the four days since Ryan and Ollison's wedding, Nikki and Evan had spoken on the phone daily, but this was the first time they'd seen each other. She tried not to read anything into that. Spring was a crazy-busy time for school staff, plus they had Noah and his schedule to consider.

Nikki had decided not to ask Evan about his mood on Sunday, reasoning that if she was going to jump, she wanted to give them every opportunity to, as her mother said, get in over their heads.

Since Sunday, she felt as if she'd turned into one of the teenagers with whom she worked at the high school—checking her phone every two minutes. *Did he call? Has he texted? Maybe he emailed. Should I text him?*

It was more than garden-variety anxiety or the energy of infatuation. The thought of hearing that yummy baritone rough with sleep in the morning or languid and dreamy at night lit all her senses on fire. She craved it. During the day, she wanted to know what was happening in his world. He'd long been a touchstone for her, the person she called to ground her day and settle her emotions. Unruly students and angry teachers stressing her out? A text exchange with Evan (heavy on the Bitmojis) could have her laughing in seconds. Now there was the added delicious tension of passion.

Unbridled, incomparable, hungry passion.

When Evan had failed to text her on Monday, Nikki had spent her lunch hour in the noble pursuit of looking up synonyms for *desire.*

Craving, eagerness, fascination, lust (oh, yeah), *need, passion, thirst...* It all fit.

Monday night, Evan had called her at home and invited her to his place "whenever you can get here after school on Wednesday."

I can get there on Tuesday, she'd wanted to say, but checked herself.

After school assembly Tuesday morning, Minn had called her into the principal's office and demanded, "What happened this weekend? You look like you swallowed a heart-eyes emoji."

Nikki had laughed. It had *felt* as if she'd swallowed a heart-eyes emoji, but she wasn't prepared to share any info. It was all too new, too fragile and vulnerable. She hadn't even told Evan that she was officially falling in love with him.

"Dad, can Aunt Nikki come to my practice on Saturday?"

"That's up to Aunt Nikki." Evan turned his head toward her. "Aunt Nikki, would you like to attend my son's Pee Wee practice—"

"Don't call it Pee Wee, Dad! It's *baseball*."

Evan gave Nikki the most adorable wry look. "My bad. Wanna watch this kid's baseball practice with me?"

Nikki nearly clapped with eagerness but cautioned herself to play it at least a little cool. "I'd love to."

Happy, Noah reached for a giant handful of popcorn and crammed every kernel into his mouth at once.

"Hey, slow down!" Evan ordered. Though he

never spoke to his son without an undercurrent of love, Nikki heard the unusual tension in his voice and noted again the tightness in his shoulders that had been there since Sunday at the hotel.

"I'm going to start dinner."

"Wha-r-wa-ha-wa?" Noah asked with his mouth still full.

"Don't talk when your mouth is stuffed with food. In fact, don't stuff your mouth with food at all," Evan said as he rose from the sofa. "It's a safety issue, in addition to suggesting you've been poorly parented."

Sucking noisily on the water bottle his father had filled earlier, Noah said, "What's that mean?"

"It means get ready to hop into the shower while I start dinner. We'll challenge Aunt Nikki to Wii bowling after we eat. High score gets an extra scoop of ice cream for dessert *and* picks a movie to watch."

"O-*kay*!" Noah scrambled to his feet, savvy enough not to argue about bath time when dessert and a movie hung in the balance.

"I'll be up in a sec to get you started," Evan promised.

"'Kay 'kay!" Noah took off at his usual gallop.

He was halfway up the stairs when Evan added, "Socks go *in*side the laundry hamper."

So far it was an ordinary night at home, but for Nikki it brought a familiar magic. Family life was a collective of details that comprised the big picture.

Her parents had worked in unison to turn mundane details like this one into moments that lived in their children's hearts. Nikki and her sibs couldn't remember every situation, but they remembered the feelings. That's what she wanted to give her own family someday.

"I thought I'd sauté some chicken breasts and make rice. You okay with that?" Evan asked her.

"You look tired," she said honestly, rising and crossing to him. "Was it a hard day?"

She'd caught him off guard. His eyes told her something was bothering him, but all he'd cop to was, "Busy week."

A frisson of misgiving uncoiled in her chest as she thought of him standing by the window in their hotel room, his mind miles away, his handsome shoulders rigid. If they hadn't moved from friendship to more, would he have confided in her? Would she have asked?

"Daaaad, I'm ready!"

Evan wiped a hand across his face. "That means he's buck naked and about to get water everywhere."

"Okay. Let's order pizza," Nikki said spontaneously.

Relief flared in Evan's tired eyes, quickly replaced by determination. "I promised you dinner. I make a great chicken piccata."

"I order an excellent pizza. And for the record, pizza *is* dinner."

A grateful and endearingly sheepish single-dad smile curved his lips. "We ordered a good one from Gigantesco Sunday night. Best I've had around here."

"I've never eaten there."

"They've only been in business a year, and you've been mostly carb-avoidant for the past two." Reaching for a strand of black hair that had fallen free from her fishtail braid, he seemed to study it, like he would a painting. "I'm glad you can be you when we're together."

Was hair an erogenous zone? 'Cause Nikki was starting to feel a little frisky. Winding her arms around his neck, she pressed close. "I'm glad, too. How're you going to feel about it when I'm soft and squishy? I've already gained five pounds since I stopped Leaning Up with NorthrUp."

A grin replaced the preoccupied expression from earlier. "This Northrup liked your body just fine the way it was." Reaching around her, he allowed his hands to wander from her low back to her bottom. "We made love the first time before you started the ultimate workouts, and you didn't hear me complain. I thought you were hot the day we met."

Damn. "Excellent answer. You're going to get lucky tonight, mister."

His grin grew. She kissed his cheek, his jaw, his neck before he swooped down and claimed her mouth. Total bliss. Why on Earth hadn't she been aware enough to continue what they'd started two years ago? Her would-be wedding was two weeks away; it could have been theirs.

On the other hand, they had two years of best friendship under their belts—an excellent foundation by any measuring stick.

When the kiss ended, she snuggled into his chest and his arms tightened around her, his heart a strong and steady thump beneath her ear. They had some things to work through, of course: big things. But they were on their way. He'd just admitted he'd been attracted to her from the day they'd met! As for her...

"Why are you laughing?" Evan murmured onto the top of her head.

"Because after six years of college and a whole lot of therapy, it turns out Mother knows best."

"About?"

"How to get across the Red Sea."

Still holding her, Evan leaned back to look at her face. "Want to explain that?"

"Daaaaad!" Noah hollered from upstairs. "Where are you? I'm a naked man!"

Nikki laughed harder. "Go upstairs." She stepped out of Evan's arms. "I'll order a pizza. Do you have salad veggies?"

"I do but wait till I come down." He kissed her forehead. "We'll make it together."

The promise to take her to Paris tonight on a

chartered jet would not have made her happier. This was exactly what she craved—an average night at home with the man and child she loved.

"What's wrong?" Evan asked, his gaze narrowing. "You gasped."

"Did I?" Her heart was beating a beat a mile a minute. *The man and child she loved.* Not *was falling in love with*: she was there—full dive, in way over her head. And she had no intention of climbing out. Taking a breath, she calmed her heartbeat. "Nothing's wrong. I just…"

She'd just realized she'd found her *bashert*—that once-in-a-lifetime, meant-to-be love. Her mother had hit the nail on the head: Deep in her heart, Nikki had always known it was Evan. That's why she had run away so fast.

"I'm sorry I ducked out on us two years ago," she told him, her voice froggy but sincere. He looked surprised.

One large palm cupped her jaw. "I'm sorry I let you."

"Daa-aad!"

"Okay, go!" She pushed lightly on Evan's chest. "Take care of your naked little man." She held on to his shirt for just a second longer. "Later," she added quietly but with great promise, "I'm planning to take care of my big naked man."

Pizza and games, laughter and a movie, then tucking a sleepy boy into bed…

Wine and kissing and soft conversation...and more kissing (along with upper body privileges)... then walking upstairs and tiptoeing past Noah's room on the way to Evan's...

It all made for a wonderful night.

"We have school tomorrow," Nikki murmured, hugging Evan's arm more tightly around her waist as they spooned.

"I know. Believe me, I'm wondering how I'm going to teach literary devices in classic American literature when my mind is on erotica." He growled into her neck.

Laughing then remembering that Noah was a room away, she shushed herself and rolled over inside his embrace. Facing him she whispered, "Tonight was perfect."

Evan kissed the tip of her nose. "Sorry about dinner. I know," he said before she could rebut. "Pizza is dinner. That's no way to go courting, though."

Nikki shivered with delight. "Evan Bradley Northrup, are you courting me?"

Evan hesitated. "We're dating."

Ruh roh.

The attempt to deflect her question sounded very much like Prince Charles responding, "Whatever love is" when asked whether he and a very young Lady Di had truly fallen for each other. And the whole world knew how that had turned out.

Courting had a clear connotation: the word implied a couple was headed toward something permanent. Dating...not so much.

"I suppose," she said carefully, "it would seem a little early to put a definition on a relationship that's only a few days old."

The streetlamp outside his bedroom window cast enough light for her to see him frown. "Yeah. I suppose."

"Then again, our relationship is *two years* and a few days old," Nikki added. "When should we take this into the daylight?"

"What do you mean?"

"With Noah. We can't keep sneaking around. I mean, we can, but I don't want to. Do you?" She smiled, trying to convince herself that Evan, too, wanted their relationship to proceed full-steam-ahead, even though every brain cell in her body told her his brakes were locked. "Maybe I'm flattering myself, but I think Noah's going to be pretty stoked when he finds out you and I are together."

Evan froze. *And there you go*, she realized, the sensation of his pulling away even as he remained utterly still impossible to miss.

Nikki sat up, wrapping the sheet and blanket around her. She pushed a hand through her hair. "I just got a strong feeling I'm not going to be storing a toothbrush here." Evan followed her up, his back against the headboard. Nikki turned her head to look back at him.

"I didn't say that," he said. "Nik…this is new."

He's right. Leave him alone. Don't push it. But another part of her, a strong and savvy part, knew Evan's resistance wasn't as simple as wanting to take this new part of their relationship more slowly.

Leaning over to turn on the bedside lamp, she let her eyes and her mind adjust a moment. It would be easier to be vulnerable in the dark, but she needed to see his face clearly. "When I went to see my mother Sunday morning, I was scared. She told me that love, all love, is like water too deep for your feet to touch the bottom and too fast to swim in. And I realized I'd never been in love like that, the kind of love I couldn't control…until you. I'm not in this to date and then figure out how to go back to being friends when we burn out. I don't want to burn out with you. Ever."

Phew. Granted, no relationship expert in the world would suggest lobbying for forever on the second "date," but it was far from the beginning of their relationship. She'd spent years running after the wrong thing, which basically amounted to standing still. She didn't have the patience to waste more time in her life.

"I'm thirty-seven," she claimed, feeling a strength she hadn't felt before, "and I know what I want."

If at that point Evan had said, *I'm nuts about you, but I need to go slowly. Let's work through it together*, she'd have kept the faith and pressed on to the far shore. But he didn't say that. Evan said nothing at all.

The rise and fall of his chest told her his breath was shallow and strained. The blue eyes that twinkled at her in humor, softened in empathy when she was upset and smoldered with desire were now shuttered and impossible to read.

She'd jumped, but he was still standing on the shore.

They'd already spent time becoming best friends and had made love the first time a little over two years ago. The attraction had been there all along. Some questions, like *Are you still emotionally bound to Noah's mother and what are you going to do about that?* should have been addressed right away. She'd just assumed...

"I've never asked you much about Mikaela. Discussing her seemed uncomfortable for you, so I let it go and instead formed some assumptions of my own."

Evan's brow lowered. "Such as?"

Nikki's heart thumped in warning against her chest. *This is a very poor choice for pillow talk.* She carried on anyway. One way or another, she had to know: Was this the real thing, or was she lying to herself again? "Such as..." She rubbed her forehead, feeling a headache coming on. "I don't know. You never talk about your marriage. It's been shrouded in mystery. Sometimes I wonder if it's like a shield for you."

"A shield."

"So you can keep your relationships with women at arm's length."

Immediately Evan's jaw tightened. "Can we leave Mikaela out of this for now?"

Nikki shook her head sincerely. "No. See, that's exactly what I mean."

"She has nothing to do with us."

"She has everything to do with us. Your ex-marriage is a big red stop sign." Nikki wanted forever. She had to ask the hard question, as frightening as it was. "Do you want to move past your divorce? Do you want another marriage?"

He didn't want to answer—it was painfully obvious—but he did. "I've never wanted a parade of women…of mothers…through Noah's life. I still don't want that."

On a trip to the Oregon coast when she in high school, Nikki had been stung on the ankle by a jellyfish. This felt a lot like that, only on her heart. "And I don't want to be part of a parade."

"You're not." Bending his neck, Evan ran his hands through his hair. "You're not. That isn't what I meant."

He couldn't or wouldn't say more, so she asked the question with potentially the most heartbreaking answer. "Do you see me staying 'Aunt Nikki'?"

The top of Evan's head told her nothing, which, unfortunately, told her everything.

She'd pushed him, and anyone would have cautioned her that it was too much, too soon. Moving forward with the romance would be a huge mistake, however, if he couldn't picture her as anything more than his son's fictive auntie. She had no idea how to break up with him after falling in love, then go back to being his friend and Noah's aunt—only.

She didn't want to be hurt and angry with him. He'd never said he wanted everything to change between them; that was her desire. She was hurt and angry anyway.

"Daddy! Daddy, I have to go pee!"

Evan looked at her miserably.

"Go," she mouthed, holding the covers as he left the bed and stepped guiltily into a pair of sweats.

Turning to her when he reached the door, Evan clearly wanted to say something but seemed unsure.

"Daddy, this hallway is dark!" Noah's voice sounded closer now.

Nikki jumped out of bed on the opposite side, bringing the covers with her as she grabbed her own clothes.

"I'm coming, buddy," Evan called, watching her a moment longer before leaving the room and shutting the door behind him.

Tears filled Nikki's eyes as she listened to Evan escort his son to the hall bathroom. Being part of their lives was a precious part of hers. The past few days she'd been certain she was going to graduate from "Aunt Nikki" and "my best friend" to something more. Now she wondered if, after tonight, she'd be able to hang on to even one of those roles for long.

She wanted too much, too soon.

And Evan was offering too little, too late.

Chapter Thirteen

Evan rarely visited his father at the office. Even when he was a kid, he'd sensed that work was Steven's escape, the place he didn't have to pretend to be an interested husband or father.

Today Evan needed to talk to Steven alone, without interruptions. He'd made an appointment with his father's assistant—Monday ten forty-five sharp for half an hour only, per his father's packed schedule.

Seated behind his desk when Evan arrived, Steven rose, extending a hand for a brief, firm shake. "Have a seat." He gestured to the less comfortable chair across the broad desk. Steven's assistant had asked if Evan wanted coffee or tea, but Steven offered nothing. Evan doubted it crossed his father's mind.

"What brings you to Portland today?"

Evan nearly laughed at the blatant impatience in the question. He could almost hear the tick-tick-tick of the time clock inside his father's head. He decided to get straight to the point. "Northrups suck at long-term relationships. I want to know why."

What the question lacked in warmth, it made up for in surprise value. Steven reached into his desk drawer after a roll of antacids, popped two in his mouth and chewed before inquiring, "Are you expecting me to provide your answer?"

"Maybe. Did it start with your parents? Before that?"

"Does it matter?"

"It matters to me." Evan heard the combativeness in his voice. He didn't care. Unable to sit, he rose and paced the room. "I'm just wondering what it is—genetics? Relationship Deficit Disorder? The chronic inability to care about anyone more than we care about ourselves? There's something inside us, Father—inside you, me and Drew—that makes us hurt people. You know that, right? I've watched your wives cry when they realized it was over for reasons they never quite figured out."

Steven had picked up a pencil and was tracing the eraser across his desk blotter. "Only some of them cried. I've had a couple who were happier to leave with a hefty settlement."

"You really don't get it, do you? I don't want

my son to be like you. Or Drew. Or me. God forbid like me."

Steven's eyes, a more faded version of his son's, rose to meet Evan's. "What makes you think you're the worst of the lot?"

Standing in the middle of the room, feeling the plush carpet beneath the soles of his shoes, Evan realized that desperation removed the filter typically barring the truth between him and his father. "Because I had a chance. Like you and Drew never have had. I have someone who…loves me. Someone who doesn't want anything from me except to let her in. And I can't."

Steven was looking down at his desk. Did he care what Evan said? Did it matter? For once, Evan simply needed to speak the truth out loud. "I can't take the risk of loving her, because screwing it up would kill me. I can't stand the thought of hurting her or my son, because he loves her, too. And I'm never going to put him through the hell of watching mothers come and go because his father is too damaged or too weak or too pitiful to see it through."

"That's enough!" Steven broke the pencil between his fingers. He pushed himself forcefully from the desk. "Your judgment has not been lost on me through the years, Evan." Walking around the desk, he confronted his son squarely. "You're arrogant. You think what you see is all that exists. But you know nothing about my life."

"Whose fault is that?"

"All right. I'll give that to you." Crossing to a highboy against the wall, Steven opened the top drawer and withdrew what appeared to be a billfold as he continued. "You don't have to remind me that my parenting skills leave a good deal to be desired. Believe me or not, my intention was never to keep getting married. I intended for Cynthia to be my second and final wife. I thought she'd be a good mother to you."

"She was. Until you replaced her with Bettina."

"I didn't 'replace' Cynthia." Steven sounded disgusted by the idea. "If you've been dissecting my relationship as long as you appear to have, you should know that Cynthia left because I was in love with someone else when I married her. Understandably, she became tired of what she termed 'the competition I can't win.'"

Evan's thoughts skidded to a halt. "I don't remember a woman before Cynthia."

"I know. You were too young. I should have talked about her more, but…" Steven's thumb moved idly across the leather of the wallet-sized item he held. After taking several steps forward, he handed it to Evan. Opening it, unsure of what he would find, Evan felt his heart stumble as he flipped through photos of his mother alone, his mother and father together and both of them with him as an infant.

"We were sixteen," Steven said as Evan turned

back to the first photo, the one that captured his attention the most. "She busted my chops at the Oaks Park skating rink. Your mother was there with friends of hers, and I was with a friend of mine. Some kid neither of us knew was deliberately shoved to the floor by somebody else right in front of me, and I skated around him. Beth had never skated before, but she helped the kid up then clomped after me, haranguing me about common decency and quoting Albert Einstein. 'The world will not be destroyed by those who do evil, but by those who watch them without doing anything.' I went back and made sure the kid could skate undisturbed, then got her number. We were inseparable after that."

The small smile around Steven's lips was replaced with a grief that seemed to swallow his face. Evan had never before seen an expression like that on his father's face.

"When your mother got sick," Steven said, "that, to me, seemed like an evil. I refused to believe there was nothing we could do. I wouldn't listen to her when she told me it was time to say goodbye." Pressing his thumb and index finger against his eyes in a way that appeared hard enough to hurt, he added, "I never did say it to her." When Steven looked up again, he stared wearily past Evan, unable to connect, it seemed, even now. "Noah has her smile.

That's why I find it…challenging to get to know him well."

Evan felt as if he'd entered a parallel universe where the rules were the same, but all the information had changed. His impulse was to grab his father in a hug—screw the handshakes they typically stuck to. It was so damn obvious, though, that Steven didn't want that. While Evan stood, torn, Steven spoke again.

"If you're sincere that you're in love, I would advise you not to assume you can't make it work because of faulty genetic wiring. That would be garbage in any case, and you've never struck me as someone willing to live a lie. I'd suggest instead that you ask yourself how much joy the thought of loving her brings you and whether you can accept that someday your grief may be that deep and that abiding as well."

When his voice grew hoarse with the emotion he had never once before exhibited in front of Evan, Steven rather roughly pulled the wallet of photos from his son's hands, returned it to the drawer where it lived and stood at his desk with his back to Evan.

"I think that for today," Steven said, "this meeting is adjourned."

Nikki had chosen the Oregon Garden for her wedding venue because it epitomized so much of what she loved about her home state, with twenty different botanical gardens illustrating the diverse beauty of Oregon's natural areas. She'd chosen the Garden Green and Grand Hall, which was rather formal, as the wedding and reception sites, because they offered the greatest capacity for the time of year.

Standing in the back of the hall, Nikki watched a surprising number of guests, given the short notice, dance at Gia and Todd's wedding. The DJ was as good as Nikki had originally hoped when the wedding was supposed to be hers and Drew's.

It didn't hurt at all anymore to remember that Drew had dumped her. He'd done her a big favor, though the way he'd gone about it still pissed her off a little. They'd finally gotten together to exchange the items they'd left at each other's places. She'd discovered he was dating his coworker, which aroused a whole host of questions, but what would be the point of going there at this point? There was nothing left—really, zippo—in the way of attraction on her end. She'd been unfair to him, too; if she'd known herself better at the start of their relationship, if she'd have accepted herself more, they'd never have gotten past the first couple of dates.

Their meeting had lasted all of twenty minutes. They'd chatted briefly. He'd mentioned with great enthusiasm a new HIIT training video he was working on, and when she'd noticed him looking disapprovingly at the food baby she'd been growing (with great enjoyment, she might add), Nikki had wished him a good afternoon and left. Drew was a great reminder of what happened when you abandoned yourself. She planned not to do that ever again.

Sipping her champagne by the window that looked onto the gardens, Nikki congratulated herself for bowing out of the bridal party and releasing all maid of honor duties. That really would have been an act of supreme codependence. Gia had, of course, been 100 percent understanding. Watching Gigi now as she, her husband and a couple hundred of their family and friends danced to "Somebody Loves You" by Betty Who, Nikki realized this wedding suited Gia much more than it did her. If she ever planned her own wedding again, she'd go with the Discovery Pavilion in the Rediscovery Forest—open-air, surrounded by Douglas firs and eighty people max. Or, if her husband-to-be agreed, they could schedule an "elopement" on the bridge in the Amazing Water Garden.

The thought made her cry only a little today, which was a big step ahead of where she'd been a couple of weeks ago, when she'd barely made it through a school day without bawling in the staff bathroom.

She and Evan had gone no-contact—not by any spoken or tacit agreement. He hadn't texted or called, and she wasn't ready to, either, though she'd never abruptly check out of Noah's life. She and

Evan would have to work out some sort of visitation. No child should lose someone abruptly without an explanation, although maybe Evan had already offered his son an explanation for her absence?

The thought did not sit well. Raising her glass of champagne to her lips, Nikki tried to steer her thoughts away from Evan. She'd promised herself a break from trying to analyze his reluctance to go all in with her. What she knew for sure was that she'd made the right decision for herself: As long as Evan waved the red flag of noncommittal, Nikki would honor them both by refusing to get more involved.

"You look beautiful, sweetheart."

"Dad!" Nikki almost spilled her champagne. "I didn't see you."

"No, you were far away." Sang's accepting smile was a balm to her nerves. He looked handsome, her dad, in his wedding finery, his still-thick hair freshly trimmed and peppered with attractive gray. "It's getting hot in here. Let's get some air."

"Don't you want to dance with Mom? You love Betty Who."

"She's holding Lani. We'll dance later. I'm waiting for 'Time Warp.'"

"Oh, Dad, I'm sorry. 'Time Warp' isn't on the playlist."

"It is now. Your mother slipped the DJ a Grant to put it in." Sang checked his wristwatch. "Only a little after 2:00 p.m…still plenty more dancing to come, You planned this wedding very nicely, by the way. Come on, I'm *shvitzing*."

He didn't look like he was perspiring at all, nor did it feel warm to Nikki, who nevertheless dutifully followed her father out the glass doors.

Sang hadn't said much about Nikki's supposed premature split from Evan, but she knew he was concerned because he'd already danced with her twice, ensured she was eating and kept checking up on her.

"So." Sang studied Nikki approvingly in the perfect spring sunlight. "That green is a good color on you with your black hair. Did I ever tell you that the first time I saw you, I couldn't stop looking at your eyes? So huge and dark and full of life. 'I want to show those eyes the world,' I thought." Holding out his arm to her, the way he would have today if he'd walked her down the aisle, Sang winked. "I also thought, 'She looks just like me. Gorgeous!'"

Nikki laughed. "I remember that when I was younger, everyone assumed I was Korean when I was with you."

"Yes." Sang nodded. "And I would tell them, 'No, you're mistaken. I'm Guatemalan.'" Giving her forearm a loving squeeze, he said, "You know, I don't have a recent photo of you. I'd like one for my office. Let's get the photographer to take a special portrait. In the Rose Garden. Come on, we'll scout a location."

"No!" Nikki laughed. "Daddy, this is not my wedding. It wouldn't be appropriate."

"I appreciate your concern for protocol, but the way this all came about does not follow the rules. Gia and Todd won't mind."

"Dad," Nikki said patiently but more firmly, "I am not sitting for a personal portrait today."

Looking at first as if he might argue, Sang shrugged in acquiescence. "All right, let's walk to the Rose Garden anyway."

Her father really was behaving a bit oddly today. Her mother had been, too. Several times, she'd caught them staring at her and whispering to each other. When they'd noticed her catching them at it, they'd smile broadly and go about their partying. Her little ruse with Evan, now that it was over, had probably caused them even more concern.

"The weather was perfect today, wasn't it?" Nikki commented, grateful Gia and Todd had been able to hold their ceremony outdoors as scheduled.

"Very nice." She and Sang made small talk as they strolled past the area recently used for the ceremony. Just beyond it was a lovely view of the Willamette Valley and the Rose Garden that appeared to be her dad's target. After a brief discussion about the food at the reception, Sang commented conversationally, "Mom filled me in on the details about Evan. Have you thought about him much today?"

Nikki nearly stumbled in her stiletto sandals.

Stopping to regain her bearings, she downed the contents of her champagne glass then asserted with great wisdom and self-control, "I'd rather not talk about Evan."

"Humor me."

"Oy. Dad."

"If it means anything, we all think you make a wonderful couple."

"Dad, please. Mom already gave me this whole spiel about the Red Sea and how I had to be the first one to jump into the raging waters of love. Well, I jumped. But I was in the water alone and now I just want to forget about it."

"Evan has his own fears. Everyone does."

"I know. But fear can kill opportunity."

"Yes, if we let it."

Continuing to hold his daughter's arm, Sang began to walk again. Nikki didn't want to go to the Rose Garden anymore, or to return to the wedding. A tear fell silently down her cheek, and she knew there were plenty more ready to follow. Dear lord, she wanted to be alone.

"I think Evan wants to get past his fear. Maybe all he needs is another chance."

"Dad, come on, stop. You don't know that."

"I do." Sang nodded, indicating that Nikki should look ahead. "*He* told me."

Standing beneath an arbor twined with climbing rose vines, a man in a midnight blue suit stood, looking at her.

"I didn't call him. He called your mother and me," Sang assured as Evan started toward them. Giving his daughter's arm a reassuring squeeze, he said with great caring, "There's no rule that says you can't jump twice. If it feels right."

As Evan approached, Sang turned and walked in the direction from which they'd come. Nikki could hardly wrap her brain around what was going on here, much less what she felt beneath the confusion. One thing she was certain of, however: hurt or not, angry or not, when she saw Evan Northrup in a suit with his wavy hair combed back and his blue eyes intense and searching, it had the power to make her weak in the knees.

"Walk with me?" He held out a hand to help her across the grass in her heels, but she needed her wits about her. Touching him was not conducive to keeping a clear head.

Reaching for the long skirt of her full-length dress, Nikki then lifted it as she walked beside him.

She felt his gaze on her, steady and intent. "If you're furious with me, I don't blame you," he said. "I'm furious with me, too. I actually looked through classic novels, trying to find a script for telling someone who means the world to you you're sorry you hurt them."

Someone who means the world to you. That put

a chink in her defenses. Keeping her gaze on the grass, she mumbled, "What did you come up with?"

"Not much. None were groveling enough. And when you've screwed up as much as I have, a little groveling seems to be in order."

They reached the rose arbor, where Evan stopped, continuing to look at Nikki, who pretended to study the skyline.

"Nikki, I'm so damn sorry for what I said about a parade of mothers walking through Noah's life. You could never be part of that. You're the one person besides me I'd trust with his life."

The words *I love you* might not have had more of an impact. The one thing Nikki had never doubted, would never doubt, was the deep, fierce, all-encompassing love Evan had for his son. Looking at him, she nodded. "Thank you," she said and meant it.

Evan shifted his weight then shoved his hand through his hair, ruining its careful brushing. "I rehearsed and rehearsed what I want to say to you." He shook his head. "What an idiot. I keep thinking I can control this thing."

Her heart started to pound. Hard. He was so nervous.

"What 'thing'?" she asked, deeply unsure whether she wanted to hear the answer today of all days.

He looked at her as if the question surprised him. "This." He gestured between them. "This... love thing, Nik."

She stopped breathing.

His hand made another trip through his hair. At that moment, Nikki longed to reach up and finger comb it for him or give him a hug and tell him she loved him, but he already knew where she stood in their relationship; she still wasn't sure what he wanted. She forced herself to wait.

Evan started to perspire. "I teach literature. I've read the classic love stories. You'd think I wouldn't suck at this."

She couldn't help smiling as she shrugged. He really was adorable. With each bead of nervous perspiration that appeared on his forehead, her fears began to evaporate. "It's easier to read a love story than to write one."

"True words." Evan reached for both her hands, and she felt them trembling. "You scare the hell out of me." She'd take that as a compliment. "You said I used my marriage to shield myself. You don't know how right you are. Mikaela and I never pretended to love each other. We'd both hit thirty, thought we should be married but didn't want to love anyone enough to get hurt. We had no clue what marriage meant. Or what love demands. I didn't learn that until we had Noah."

The more Evan spoke, the less his hands trembled in hers.

"She and I made this incredible kid together, but that's the only legacy from our marriage, Nikki." He looked down, swallowed hard and seemed to steel himself for what he had to say next. "The morning after Ryan's wedding…after you and I made love… while you were at your parents' place, I got a call from a lawyer telling me Mikaela had passed away."

Every thought, every word got stuck inside Nikki. She made a futile attempt to slow her heart rate and disentangle her thoughts, but the only word she could come up with was, "How?"

"In an accident at a work site in Costa Rica. Almost a year ago. She left some things to Noah, so her lawyer found us. My first thought was to tell you, but…"

"You must be so worried about Noah."

"I was. I am. I've done a lot of thinking lately." He shook his head. "No, not 'thinking.' Soul searching. And what I've realized is being afraid of pain is the same of being afraid to live. I can't protect Noah from feeling the pain I felt growing up, because that's saying I want to protect him from living. I can walk with him through life, through whatever it throws at us. You were right that I used my former marriage to keep people out. To keep you out. You're the one woman I could see forever with. And I was convinced I'd screw it up."

"You're the one person I couldn't see forever with," she told him, "because I wanted it too much to let myself even imagine it."

They stared at each other in awe and then Nikki added, "I guess we're both kind of broken."

"I guess so."

"We could run away now. Or stay and figure out if the broken pieces fit together just right."

"I'm all done running," Evan said definitively. "The pain of losing someone never killed me, but trying to run from the pain almost cost me you. My father helped me realize that."

"Steven?" Her surprise was evident and possibly a little insulting, but Evan smiled.

"Yeah. I'll tell you about it later. For now…" After bringing one of her hands to his lips, he kissed it. "I was supposed to be your plus one at this wedding. I've spent the past two weeks asking myself if I can be the man you deserve by your side. I talked to my father, and I spoke to your family, too."

Now that was a surprise. "My family? My mom and dad, you mean?"

Evan shook his head. "Everyone. I wanted their blessing to do this right."

"What do you—"

Evan dropped to one knee. Continuing to hold her left hand, he released the other to reach into his inside breast pocket. "We've been dancing around each other for too long. But I think I knew from the day we met that I needed you in my life. Not just 'wanted' you, Nikki. *Needed* you. Like I need Noah to make my heart beat.

"I'm a good student and a decent teacher, but I've got a lot to learn about love." He held out a diamond set in a band of sparkling smaller diamonds. "Nikki Choi, will you let me study with you? I want to be your friend for life. And your plus one forever. Marry me. Please."

This time, hers was the hand that was shaking. Shocked and breathless, she whispered. "Okay." It wasn't nearly loud enough. "Yes," she tried again. "Yes, I will!"

Cheers and applause erupted as Evan slipped the lovely engagement ring onto her finger. Nikki reached for his face so she could kiss the heck out of it, but—

Wait…cheers and applause? She turned in the direction of the sound.

"Kiss! Kiss! Kiss!"

Her father, mother, Gia, Todd, June, Lev (holding baby Lani) and about two hundred guests filled the Garden Green, where Gia and Todd had recently said "I do." Best of all, Noah stood in front of Nikki's dad, with Sang's hands on the little boy's shoulders as Noah bounced up and down.

"She said she'd marry us, Dad!" Noah said excitedly to the crowd's delight. "See? I told you she loves us!"

Nikki was afraid her heart might burst. She stared openmouthed at Evan, who was standing now, looking at her with all the mischief and all the sunshine she loved in his sky blue eyes.

"You must have been pretty sure of yourself, mister, to gather that audience."

Bringing both her hands to his lips, Evan corrected the assumption. "I was sure about *you*. Besides, you're worth the risk."

In the next instant, Noah barreled into them, chattering about going on a "moon" together at Disneyland. The feel of him and his easy love made Nikki quite sure she had more than any one person could ask for in this life.

More cheers and whistling ensued as Evan and Nikki obeyed the request to kiss.

Back when this day was supposed to be the beginning of her forever, Nikki had hired the wedding photographer whose camera now whirred and clicked busily.

With one arm around Evan's neck and one hand on Noah's head, Nikki smiled at her family, especially connecting with Gia, who applauded and beamed with joyful tears, obviously not bothered that her big sis had just gotten engaged at her baby sister's wedding. Still, Nikki would make it up to her and Todd, maybe send them out to a fabulous dinner on her. As for her own celebration...

"I have an idea," she said for Evan's ears alone.

"What is it?" he murmured, kissing her temple... and her cheek...and her neck.

Shivers ran up and down her body. "When the time comes, let's elope with Noah."

Nodding wholeheartedly, Evan laughed. He nodded toward the crowd that waited to congratulate them. "We might get some resistance."

"True." She sighed. "Oh, well. Let's get out of here as soon as we can, though. I want some alone time with my husband and son-to-be. Hey, I just realized: Now I'm going to be your plus one. For movies, for Oaks Park, for Disneyland. For…ever."

Before this moment, Nikki hadn't realized joy could be as fiery, as fierce as passion. The fire was bright and strong now in her own heart and on Evan's handsome face when he responded, "I like the sound of that. I like the sound of that a lot."

* * * * *

COMING NEXT MONTH FROM

HARLEQUIN®
SPECIAL EDITION™

#2935 THE MAVERICK'S MARRIAGE PACT
Montana Mavericks: Brothers & Broncos • by Stella Bagwell

To win an inheritance, Maddox John needs to get married as quickly as possible. But can he find a woman to marry him for all the wrong reasons?

#2936 THE RIVALS OF CASPER ROAD
Garnet Run • by Roan Parrish

When heartbroken Bram Larkspur finds out the street he's just moved onto has a Halloween decorating contest, he thinks it's a great way to meet people. He isn't expecting to meet Zachary Glass, the buttoned-up architect across the street who resents having competition...and whom he's quickly falling for.

#2937 LONDON CALLING
The Friendship Chronicles • by Darby Baham

Robin Johnson has just moved to London after successfully campaigning for a promotion at her job and is in search of a new adventure and love. After several misfires, she finally meets a guy she is attracted to and feels safe with, but can she really give him a chance?

#2938 THE COWGIRL AND THE COUNTRY M.D.
Top Dog Dude Ranch • by Catherine Mann

Dr. Nolan Barnett just gained custody of his two orphaned grandchildren and takes them to the Top Dog Dude Ranch to bond, only to be distracted by the pretty stable manager. Eliza Hubbard just landed her dream job and must focus. However, they soon find the four of them together feels a lot like a family.

#2939 THE MARINE'S CHRISTMAS WISH
The Brands of Montana • by Joanna Sims

Marine captain Noah Brand is temporarily on leave to figure out if his missing ex-girlfriend's daughter is his—and he needs his best friend Shayna Wade's help. Will this Christmas open his eyes to the woman who's been there this whole time?

#2940 HER GOOD-LUCK CHARM
Lucky Stars • by Elizabeth Bevarly

Rory's amnesia makes her reluctant to get close to anyone, including sexy neighbor Felix. But when it becomes clear he's the key to her memory recovery, they have no choice but to stick very close together.

YOU CAN FIND MORE INFORMATION ON UPCOMING HARLEQUIN TITLES, FREE EXCERPTS AND MORE AT HARLEQUIN.COM.

HSECNM0822

He opened the mailbox absently and reached inside.
There should be an issue of *Global Architecture*. But the
moment the mailbox opened, something hit him in the
face. Shocked, he reeled backward. Had a bomb gone
off? Had the world finally ended?

He sputtered and opened his eyes. His mailbox,
the ground around it and presumably he himself were
covered in...glitter?

"What the...?"

"Game on," said a voice over his shoulder, and Zachary
turned to see Bram standing there, grinning.

"You— I— Did you—?"

"You started it," Bram said, nodding toward the
dragon. "But now it's on."

Zachary goggled. Bram had seen him. He'd seen him do something mean-spirited and awful, and had seen it in the context of a prank… He was either very generous or very deluded. And for some reason, Zachary found himself hoping it was the former.

"I'm very, very sorry about the paint. I honestly don't know what possessed me. That is, I wasn't actually possessed. I take responsibility for my actions. Just, I didn't actually think I was going to do it until I did, and then, uh, it was too late. Because I'd done it."

"Yeah, that's usually how that works," Bram agreed. But he still didn't seem angry. He seemed…impish.

"Are you…enjoying this?"

Bram just raised his eyebrows and winked. "Consider us even. For now." Then he took a magazine from his back pocket and handed it to Zachary. *Global Architecture.*

"Thanks."

Bram smiled mysteriously and said, "You never know what I might do next." Then he sauntered back across the street, leaving Zachary a mess of uncertainty and glitter.

Don't miss
The Rivals of Casper Road by Roan Parrish,
available October 2022 wherever
Harlequin Special Edition books and ebooks are sold.

Harlequin.com

Get 4 FREE REWARDS!

We'll send you 2 FREE Books plus 2 FREE Mystery Gifts.

HARLEQUIN PLUS

Announcing a **BRAND-NEW**
multimedia subscription service
for romance fans like you!

Read, Watch and Play.

Experience the easiest way to get
the romance content you crave.

Start your **FREE 7 DAY TRIAL** at
<u>www.harlequinplus.com/freetrial</u>.

HARLEQUIN

Heartfelt or thrilling, passionate or uplifting—Harlequin is more than just happily-ever-after.

With twelve different series to choose from and new books available every month, you are sure to find stories that will move you, uplift you, inspire and delight you.

HNEWS2021

Love Harlequin romance?

DISCOVER.

Be the first to find out about promotions, news and exclusive content!

Facebook.com/HarlequinBooks

Twitter.com/HarlequinBooks

Instagram.com/HarlequinBooks

Pinterest.com/HarlequinBooks

YouTube.com/HarlequinBooks

ReaderService.com

EXPLORE.

Sign up for the Harlequin e-newsletter and download a free book from any series at **TryHarlequin.com**

CONNECT.

Join our Harlequin community to share your thoughts and connect with other romance readers!
Facebook.com/groups/HarlequinConnection